KILLER BE KILLED

BOOK II: HOMEWRECKER

WILLIAM STERLING

For Stu and Billy
High School Never Ends

If you have any topics which are off limits to you and would like to check for "trigger warnings" before reading Killer Be Killed: Homewrecker, a list of topics breached in each of my books can be found on my website:

www.thewilliamsterling.wixsite.com/

I hope this helps create a safe and comfortable reading experience for you all.

If you would rather avoid any sort of spoilers, feel free to disregard.

Prologue

Detective Ramsey stood in the middle of the Camp Tall Pine's Activity Center and stared at the ceiling, bewildered by the red mess that hung above him. The kids' arm was the only part of him that was still recognizably human. The rest of him had devolved into a misshapen clot of blood, bones, and burst organs. This kid in the rafters was the last of the counselors which his cleaning crew needed to bag and tag, but they had been standing around for almost an hour trying to figure out how.

One of the detectives had jokingly grabbed a grill scraper from the camp's kitchen, waved it around grotesquely, and somehow his insensitive joke had devolved into their best idea. Detective Smalls was arranging a ladder beneath the stinking mass of ravaged teenager now, and Detective Ramsey had to excuse himself from the room. There was no reason for him to watch.

After overseeing all eleven of the other counselors' bodies getting collected from the furthest corners of the camp, and seeing scorched, burnt, bones of the campers getting sifted from the fire pit out front, the detective didn't need ANOTHER horrific image scarred into his memory.

He could stand to walk away from this one.

His boots clumped out the front door of the cabin and the outside air hit him like a wave of relief. The sun was high, but the cool winds of Fall had dropped the temperature to something reasonable. The surrounding trees were yellow, red, and orange instead of green like they had been when the massacre took place, and a thick film of fallen leaves floated atop the camp's lake.

Those damned leaves.

They'd been the ticking clock for Detective Ramsey and his crew. If there were any more clues to be found that could have helped explain what the hell had gone down here, or how, then those clues would be lost now beneath the bed of leaves until Spring. But there couldn't be too much left. Right? The dogs had sniffed out all the bodies. Gone over the campground five separate times to make sure everybody, even every pieces of everybody, had been sniffed out. But the dogs didn't know everything to look for. Weapons. Collections of trees snapped in half by some insane act of brute strength. There were things a human eye had to see to recognize. Maybe finding *everything* was unrealistic. But Ramsey had to pray he had found enough.

He thought back to his interviews with Boone and Athena Hammond. How cagey they had been with their answers. There were things they hadn't told him. He was sure of that. But could the collection of things he'd discovered prove their truths? Call out their lies? It was all such a mess. He needed months with topographical maps, colorful strings, push pins and timelines before he'd be able to make sense of any of it.

Ramsey took a deep swig of room-temperature coffee as inside the Activities Center people shouted. A squelching noise let Detective Ramsey know that his coworkers had dislodged the mass of meat from the rafters. A big blue tarp had been draped over the hole in the roof of the Activities Center, to protect the corpse inside from the elements while their team decided how best to get it down.

It sounded like the tarp could be taken down now.

Which meant it would be his last day in this place. He'd get to head home, finally. Free himself from all of the other investigators swarming around. He felt like he couldn't work here. Too many eyes. Too many ears. Too many things slipping through the cracks. This hadn't been a clean job. Not by any stretch of the imagination. And Ramsey had his suspicions why that might be. But he would keep his mouth closed. For now. He would continue to observe. Note. Report. Until the last couple pieces of this puzzle fit into place.

Maybe he'd stop by the Hammond residence on his way. Check to make sure Boone and Athena weren't getting into any trouble. See if their stories still lined up with what they'd told him initially.

Yeah. That would be good. One more chat with them, now that he'd really had a chance to process the mess they'd left behind. Maybe this time the pair would let slip what really happened here.

Chapter One

Boone

There is a click and a whirr as the tape recorder gets up to speed. It's an old one, probably the same brand and style as Boone had when he was a kid. He liked Dr. Carver's commitment to "old school" gizmos and gadgets. It helped him feel comfortable around her. The first therapist that he'd talked to kept using things like Google Calendar and Sign Up Genius to schedule appointments. They kept recommending Boone get apps on his phone that could help to track his mental health. Boone couldn't, or maybe wouldn't, let himself get caught up in all that new age techno-wizardry. Nope. He had always been low-key, low-speed.

The tape recorder hissed once, then crackled.

"Mr. Hammond. I was hoping to see you today. Please, sit," Dr. Carver greeted and offered.

"Thanks, Doc."

"Was this appointment scheduled?"

"No. I, uh, I've just been having a really hard time so I thought I'd pop in. See if you had an hour open."

"Got it. Okay. Well lucky you, huh?"

"Yeah. Lucky me."

The silence lingered in the room for a few minutes, and the tape recorder kept turning, popping and spitting static to help fill the audible void.

"So...are you going to tell me what's wrong? What brought you in today?"

Another pause as Boone weighed his words.

"Sure, doc. Yeah. It's just...I've been having trouble recently. Feeling like everything that happened at that camp is really behind us now, you know?"

Boone took a deep breath, stalling for an extra moment to gather his thoughts.

"I thought I was moving past it, but lately every time I look at Athena, I feel this urge to grab her, hide her away. I keep seeing threats in these stupid nonsense places and events around the house. Like when Athena goes to the kitchen to make popcorn for a movie. That happened last Thursday. And the whole time she was gone I was sweating through my clothes, trying to convince myself that she was fine. The popcorn and the microwave weren't masking the sound of her being strangled or sacrificed. I burst into tears when she came back into the living room and I made a total ass of myself."

"Interesting," Dr. Carver said, but it was less of a response and more of a way to nudge Boone farther into his story.

"She thinks I'm insane."

"Has she told you that?"

"No. But I can see it in her eyes. Any time I have a breakdown in front of her, I can see her face drop. She thinks I'm overreacting. She's trying so hard to put everything behind her, and I am too, but she's just doing such a better job of it than me. How? How do kids bounce back from trauma so fast?"

"Has she really 'bounced back,' as you put it? Or is she just better at masking her damage than you are?"

Boone didn't have an immediate response to that.

"All people, but especially teenage girls, are adept at reflecting back to the world what they think everybody else wants to see. It's a survival instinct, since we're tribal in nature. Our minds have learned how to blend in, how to avoid being abandoned or ostracized by those people we need for support. We can bury all sorts of emotions and anger and fear deep down...for a time. But it all comes back up eventually. She's seeing somebody, yes?"

A pause on the recording, but Boone probably nodded his head yes, based on the way Dr. Carver continued.

"Good. But you keep an eye on her. She's struggling to make sense of the same tragedy that you are. There's no way to just sweep that under the rug completely. Keep being there for her, and she'll keep being there for you. The two of you have a good bond. Better than most fathers and daughters. Cherish that. Nurture it. Let it help rebuild the both of you."

There is a loud sniffing sound on the recording. Boone has started crying.

"Thanks, Doc. That makes sense."

"She's starting school again soon, isn't she?"

"Yeah."

"Good. Maybe these new emotions you're experiencing are tied in to that. Could it be that you're afraid to let her go again? The last time you were really apart from one another was at Camp. So maybe these surging feelings are connected to that approaching event?"

"I go to the grocery store without her. She spends a lot of time in her room alone. I give her space."

"Right. But this is different, isn't it? School is big. School is full of unknown variables. School is scary."

"But its not supposed to be."

"For her? Of course it is. She's going to have to get readjusted socially after everything she's been through."

"I meant for me. It's not supposed to be scary for me."

"Every parent gets nervous when they bring their kid to school for the first time."

"But this isn't the first time. She's going to high school. I've been dropping her off at school for almost a decade now."

"Never like this though. Never after what you both just went through at the camp. Boone, I want you to take a deep breath and repeat the mantra back to me."

A hissing sound on the tape recorder as Boone draws in the prescribed breath.

"Healing takes time. Healing takes patience. I'm not okay. But I'll be okay."

"Exactly. You don't need to be 'okay' with this event coming up. If it scares you, then that's perfectly natural. But you have to accept this hurdle for what it is, and you have to be patient with yourself."

"Got it. Right. Thanks doc."

"How's your project going?"

"The basement? It's good. I've almost got all the walls…"

"No, Boone. The other project."

We hear the creak of old leather as Boone shifts in his seat.

"Oh. Yeah. I haven't touched it. Not in a few weeks."

Another long pause as Dr. Carver waits for Boone to be honest with her.

"Alright, alright, alright, doc. I rifled through everything again yesterday. But I didn't do anything. I didn't go anywhere or do any more research or anything like that. The box is just sitting there in my closet."

"You know I'm not going to force you to give that up. But we have agreed it may not be the healthiest coping skill for you at this time. But Boone, is the closet really the best place for that? It's too easy to access. Too omnipresent in your life. I want to do something here. Do you see the box every time you go to change clothes in the morning?"

"Yes."

"And do you understand why that's a problem?"

"Yes."

"You're like an addict working at a liquor store. You need to nest better. Turn your safe space into a safe place both mentally as well as physically."

"Yeah. The basement is..."

"No. Not the basement. Your whole house. The closer you keep that box, the longer your healing will take because you aren't letting go. One of these days we're going to have to cut you off cold turkey."

"But not today?"

"No. You're not ready yet."

"I'm not, Doc. I'm really not. But okay. What do I do until our next real session? Just try not to think about Athena going to school?"

"No. On the contrary. I want you thinking about that as much as possible. Normalize it. Get to the point where thinking about her leaving doesn't make you break out in sweats."

"Like I am now?"

"Just like you are now."

Dr. Carver and Boone Hammond both chuckle at that.

"Get your calendar out now though. Let's make sure we're both on the same page about when you're coming back."

The tape recorder clicked off. The session ended.

Chapter Two

Athena

For years, the Hammond residence had felt too big for Athena. Her parents had bought the place when her mom was still alive, and while the prospect of Athena having a bunch of little brothers or sisters running around was still on the table. It had two stories and an unfinished basement. It was located in a nice, quiet neighborhood in the bowels of suburbia.

It was perfect.

But then mom died and, growing up with just Athena and her father, the space had seemed cavernous. Bedrooms intended for siblings two and three became a toy room for Athena and an office for her father. Not that a firefighter had much use for a home office. The basement had remained unfinished, relegated to a storage space for all of Athena's mother's things which Boone couldn't bring himself to look at, but also couldn't bring himself to part with.

Athena had often wondered why her father didn't just sell the house. Downsize and get some extra money in their pockets. They didn't need all this room.

Or, at least, Athena had thought they didn't.

But now, after the summer she'd just had, the place instead felt too small. Cramped. Like a cage that she was desperate to escape. It had taken her months to recover, and honestly, she still wasn't sure she was totally back to herself, but she was sick and tired of being cooped up in this place. She needed to be released back into the world. She missed friends. She missed distractions.

Whoever thought that isolation and "time to herself" was good for her recovery was an idiot. Alone in the house, Athena found herself constantly cornered by her thoughts. There was nothing to focus on except her memories of Jolene; of those masks at the bonfire; of Elena, cut to pieces, the red glow of the flames dancing across her blood-slicked cheeks and her empty, blank eyes.

She couldn't take another night with those ghosts.

Athena had convinced her therapist that she was ready to reenter society.

School, to be precise.

But her dad was still being dodgy about the whole idea. Whereas Athena felt the need to get out, to spread her wings again, her father seemed to have bunkered down in their home. He was finally giving the basement some attention, but he was using it to build a damn panic room. "Just in case," he kept saying, as if the various "cases" that could go wrong were self explanatory. To her father, the house was becoming his shell. His fortress. The place he could control, so the place that he wouldn't dare leave.

The only difference between Athena's prison and Boone's bunker was the purpose of the lock.

Athena rolled over on her bed and thumbed open her phone.

Three text messages awaited her, all from Shelley.

"Today's the day!"

"Rise and shine, bitch!"

"Seriously. Are you still asleep?"

Athena glanced at the time near the top of the phone's display. 8 in the morning. She could still make it to school on time, what was Shelley worrying about?

Through the floor below her, something slammed and shook the house. Athena grabbed the edges of her mattress out of reflex, reminded of the boom she'd felt as she was electrocuted to death at camp. Her breath caught in her throat and tears instantly sprung to her eyes. She thought of the totem pole, looming large overhead and imagined Jolene with a chainsaw, leaping suddenly towards her.

But that was stupid, Athena told herself. It was just her dad in the basement, hammering something or dropping a board or whatever.

Athena exhaled and tried to regain her composure, thankful, for once, that she was alone. She'd have to control her startle reflex once she was back at school. If she jumped at every bang or thump, the kids were bound to make fun of her. They might be bound to make fun of her anyhow.

"The Dead Kid."

"Freshman Final Girl"

"Camp Tall Pines Zombitch"

She'd rolled countless possible nicknames around in her head, but knew that whatever she came up with, her peers would come up with something vastly more cruel. She remembered how Middle School had been, and she'd seen the reports about Tall Pines on the news.

The press was still keeping most of the details of the massacre on the down low. Whether because the Feds didn't know what to make of them, or because they DID know what to make of them and didn't want the public to panic, Athena didn't know. But basically the only thing that had been reported was that there had been a massacre at the camp, and that Athena and Boone had been the only survivors.

Internet Sleuths had taken the ball and run with it from there.

There were conspiracies that Athena and Boone themselves had been the ones who committed the massacre. Which was...you know...partially true. Ish. But other sleuths had stumbled on the wolf masks. Had picked up on the thread that some organized group of teenagers had come together and had something to do with all the deaths. Although what their involvement had been, nobody seemed certain.

It took every ounce of Athena's restraint not to jump on the message boards to help the theories along. She could have name dropped Jolene. She could have told them about the summoning ritual at the bonfire. The internet people seemed smart. They could piece things together from there, maybe give Athena herself a more holistic perspective on what had happened.

But no.

Athena and her father had signed NDAs the moment they got picked up by that police car. They had been stumbling down the highway together, soaked in blood, and gods, how many cars had driven past them before somebody finally called in about them?

Their rescue had been followed by a week of questioning and interrogations, starting with questions about what happened, but followed by accusations after some cops actually arrived at the scene at Tall Pines and radioed in what they were looking at.

Athena and her father stuck to their scripts, just like they'd agreed upon while they were walking. Athena was honest about everything up until the point where her father walked out of the woods at the bonfire. "Then the world just went black." The police and medical examiners chalked it up to passing out from shock. She'd fallen back into the totem pole and been zapped. Boone had conducted CPR. That was the end of it.

Athena's dad had to be much more careful with his story. He had returned to camp to save his daughter after his tire blew. He'd killed the first counselor at the Welcome Center, then...well...he couldn't exactly tell them he'd been possessed by a demon and gone on a video-game-level killing spree, could he?

He admitted to fighting some of the cultists on a rampage to save his daughter, but said the details were hazy. He'd been in a fugue state or something like that. All of the wildest kills, he hadn't been around for. A body had been literally ripped in half? Wow. That was incredible. One of the cultists must have done it during their pseudo-civil war. A body had been left gored at the top of a pike? Jeez one of the cultists must have been strong to get them all the way up there. Or maybe multiple cultists worked together? How was Boone to know?

He had dodged and feigned away from the cops' questions like a prize fighter, leaving them confused and suspicious, but unable to wrap their heads fully around how Boone could have reasonably been the culprit. Eventually the police's questions devolved into ludicrous, broad, untargeted statement-questions along the lines of "This was fucking sick. What the fuck happened? What the actual fuck happened?"

Athena's dad was a suspect still, to be sure. But not a plausible one. There was no way one person had caused so much carnage.

So the police eventually had to give up the ghost and they left Athena and her dad alone.

The hospital prescribed therapy for the pair of them and the state stationed a cop to monitor their house for the next month. They claimed it was just to make sure there was no blowback to all of this while they cleaned up the mess at camp, but Athena knew it was also to make sure they didn't make a run for it. Flee to Canada or whatever.

Athena swung her legs around the side of her bed and stood.

"I'm up now, shut up!" she texted Shelley.

Her friend's response came lightning fast. Teenage girls and their cell phones. The speeds their fingers flew defied physics.

"Hell yeah. Throw on your first day of school outfit and some war paint and get to first period. There's a seat right next to me that Timmy Horton's been trying to take ALL YEAR. I need your beautiful bubble butt to fill it!"

Athena smiled and stretched as she stood. She threw on the outfit which she'd picked the night before. Red top. Cutoff jeans. A pair of red Converse to match the top. She wandered out of her bedroom and down the steps, texting as she went.

In the kitchen she slipped two bagels into the toaster and pulled some orange juice from the fridge. She caught a glimpse of herself in the reflection of the metal fridge door as it swung closed and for a just moment saw the version of herself that had crawled away from Camp.

Cutoff jeans. But cut off by what? A scythe?

Red top. Blood?

Was she leaning into this final girl thing intentionally? The world may never know.

The bagels popped and Athena tried to turn her mind back off. She was wearing red because she liked red. Always had. She was wearing cutoff jeans because she thought she looked good in them. Shut up, brain. Shut up, brain. Shut up, brain.

Her dad came up from the basement as she scooped out a swath of cream cheese and spread it.

Boone coughed, loudly, to announce his presence as he entered the room. He had accidentally snuck up on Athena one too many times since they got home, scaring the shit out of her. The last time she'd swung a curling iron within an inch of his face.

"Morning, Dad," Athena said this time, her eyes and most of her attention remaining focused on the bagel-in-progress.

"Morning, sunshine."

Athena rolled her eyes at the nickname.

"How's the basement coming along?"

Boone glanced back towards the door he had just come up.

"Good. Good. Insulation is packed nice and tight. Should be almost totally soundproofed by now. Just gotta find a reliable guy to talk to about installing a blast door." Boone nodded, mostly to himself, and smiled. "You know anybody that's good at installing triple-locking metal doors?"

It was a joke. Just not a particularly good one, so Athena responded with nothing more than an eye roll.

"Well, ask around school. I'm willing to negotiate costs."

Doubling down on the joke? That was...a choice. Athena countered with an audible groan. Her dad had been working on that basement on and off since they returned home. He seemed convinced that the cult from Camp Tall Pines would come back, try to finish the job they had started by offing Athena. And as concerning as that idea was, Athena was weirded out by her dad's insistence that a panic room was the best way to protect them.

What if she wasn't attacked at home? What if they came for her at school?

Or what if they attacked her while she was upstairs, in her room, blocking off her access to the panic room? What if they used the room to their advantage and locked themselves in there with Athena? The whole concept of a panic room felt misguided and unhelpful. But it was keeping her dad busy. Giving him something to do besides sitting around, thinking about her maybe being murdered. So for that, at least, the room seemed to be a good thing. Athena mostly avoided mocking it. Mostly.

"Speaking of school. You ready?"

"Just about. I'll eat this really quick, then the bus'll be here in 10. I've got notebooks and pens and I think everything else I need already packed in my bag."

"You know that's not what I meant. Not your things. Are you ready?"

Athena took a big bite of her bagel, buying a few seconds to dodge the question.

Was she ready?

She was going to be an outcast. A freak. Normal kids were scared of their first day of high school. Scared of not fitting in, not having anything in common with their classmates. So how bad was ATHENA going to have it? A month late to classes, camera crews following her around, police escorts, and the stories about her...Gods, the stories. Somehow rumors of the demon had escaped the camp. Shelley had warned Athena about the gossip via text, asked if any of the rumors were true. Something supernatural had happened at that camp, hadn't it? It wasn't just a bunch of weird kids killing other kids, was it?

Athena hadn't answered. How could she?

So was she ready for school? Hell no. But at least by going to school she would have a CHANCE at normalcy. She craved a return to her old routine. Go to classes. Do her work. See some friends. Hell, even dealing with bullies and gossip, as awful as that could be, would feel welcome compared to the isolated hell that her house had become.

"Of course," Athena said to her dad, forcing the most genuine smile she could muster despite her complicated feelings.

It seemed to work. Her dad nodded and glanced back at the door to the basement.

"You sure you don't want me to drive you? It wouldn't be any trouble. There's a ton to do downstairs, but it could wait. If you wanted."

Athena smiled sadly at her dad. She wanted to make a joke about how poorly things had gone the last time he dropped her off anywhere. Typical teenager behavior maybe. Making a joke out of the most horrific things possible. But she knew her dad wouldn't take the joke as a joke. He was still struggling to make his peace with what had happened. He wouldn't talk about it. Ever. But she could see the torment in his eyes. The wild way his focus darted away anytime a screen door slammed shut in the neighborhood. The way he became quieter, distant, any time he pulled the butcher's knife from its block in the kitchen. He wasn't right yet. Dark humor wouldn't hit with him the way it used to. Although Athena's dad had made it back from camp with her, a part of him had died that night. She was still trying to sort out how big a part of him that had been.

She downed the glass of orange juice, then bit into the second half of her bagel, gripping it in her teeth as she rushed up to her dad. She surprised him with a hug and a muffled "Luff You!"

Boone hugged her back, a little harder and a little longer than he needed to. Athena didn't begrudge him of it, though.

"Have a good day at school, sweetie."

Athena knocked knuckles with her dad and winked at him.

"Don't worry, Dad. I've got this. Anybody gives me crap I'll just bust some faces again." She tried to say their old catchphrase, but there was no telling how much of it her dad understood through her mouthful of bagel.

Athena spun on her heel, grabbed her backpack from its usual spot near the door, the same spot where it had been every day since Elementary School, and took off through the front door before her dad could see the tears welling in her eyes. She needed to look strong and confident or there was no way he'd let her go.

The door swung shut behind Athena and she turned up the street, reaching the stop sign just on time to hear the squealing of air brakes two blocks away. The big cheese was early. Behind her, the cops stationed to watch Athena's house shifted in their seats and stared out at her, clearly uncomfortable with letting one of their charges just walk away like this. But she was going to school. What were they going to do about it? Athena waggled her backpack on her shoulders, as if to show them that her intentions were good, then climbed aboard the bus when it pulled up. She sank into a hard, smelly, leather seat halfway back and then, for the first time in months, she embraced the feeling of freedom.

She had escaped her house.

She was headed back to the real world.

The tears finally came as she rested her backpack in her lap. Tears of relief over doing something 'normal' again. Tears of anxiety, not knowing how the kids at school would react to her return. Tears of sadness for the empty spot on the bus where Elena was supposed to be seated with her. Tears of longing for the part of her dad she had lost that summer.

It took most of the bus ride, but by the time the bus pulled up to Bayside High School, Athena had dried her eyes, pulled her eye liner from a side pocket of her bag, and 'concealer-ed' away any signs of her distress. The face that would reintroduce the world to Athena Hammond was the face of a survivor. No more tears. It was time to restart her life.

Chapter Three

Boone

Boone watched his daughter down the sidewalk, keeping a sharp eye on her for as long as he could. He glanced suspiciously at the police car on the other side of the street, still mistrusting their intentions. "Security" they had said when they first posted up outside his house. "Make sure those cultists don't come circling back around for you."

Boone only halfway bought that story.

He was still a suspect. So was Athena. He wasn't stupid. But being a suspect was a hindrance. A nuisance. It meant he had to be especially careful as he walked back upstairs, pulled the box from his closet, and loaded it into his truck's passenger seat in the garage. He glanced at the box again to make sure the lid was still shut. No stray flap was raised up, willing to expose its contents to a curious officer who stopped him to check in the window.

But everything was secure. Like it always was.

Boone hit the garage door button and fired up his engine as the chain pulled the garage up, revealing the harsh light of the outside world. He pulled out slowly, intentionally giving the impression that he wasn't in a rush. Just off to get some groceries, boys. No need to be alarmed. He even went so far as to nod at the officers as he passed, hoping they couldn't see the sweat dripping down his temples.

But the officers merely nodded back. Their expressions were impossible to read behind their oversized sunglasses, but the nods seemed friendly enough. For now.

Boone drove down the road and hung a left, heading towards both the grocery store and the highway simultaneously. He kept a close eye on the cars in his rearview mirror, making sure the same car didn't follow him for more than three, four blocks. He stuck his head out the driver's side window, scanned the sky overhead for a police helicopter of some sort. He didn't know how seriously the cops were taking his "security" and while a helicopter would have been some terribly obvious overkill on their part, Boone wasn't taking any chances.

But he made it to the highway without any issues. No sign of any tail as he merged into the heavy morning traffic. He let himself breathe a bit easier and opened the box in the passenger seat.

Jolene Dubanik's face glared back at him from the top page of a clipboard inside. Even in her high school yearbook picture, you could see the poison behind those eyes. Boone tried not to look too hard at the picture, but instead looked beneath it where he had scribbled the dead murderous bitch's home address. 3043 Miller Grove Court. It hadn't changed since he found it last night. He knew it hadn't, but it gave him some comfort to double check himself.

The drive slipped by without event. Boone turned on the radio and listened to a 'classic' rock station that kept playing songs Boone could remember coming out for the first time. Shit, he was old. Since when was Pearl Jam classic rock, huh?

He pulled up to Jolene's former home almost an hour later.

The place was a small, decaying ranch with walls that had once been white and a flower bed that had once had flowers. The grass was almost a foot high and the only vehicle in the driveway was a truck with no wheels. Maybe Jolene's dad had been fixing it before he died. Who knew? Who cared? All that mattered to Boone was that Jolene's mom's little red Prius was nowhere to be seen. There was a chance it was in the garage, but the last three times Boone had swung by here to scope the place out, the car had been parked right beside the truck in the driveway. Which meant today was the day. Nobody was home. Boone could finally get a look inside.

He smiled as he slipped from the driver's seat and circled around to the toolbox in the truck's bed. The backpack he pulled out was heavy. A lockpicking kit, a crowbar, some gloves and protective booties to slip over his shoes. Boone had spent the last month slowly assembling a top-notch burglars kit.

He approached the Dubanik residence indirectly, walking up the street a few houses before ducking into the woods that wound behind the house and coming back around to the place from the rear. Nobody from the street would see his approach this way. He slipped through a break in the old, unkept fence and went up to the back door with every intention of jimmying open the lock, but found a torn screen door as his only barrier. Boone shrugged, lowered his shoulder, and slipped through the damaged screen without any issues.

He was really here. Jolene's old house.

Boone made sure his excitement didn't cloud his judgment, pausing to slip on the cloth shoe coverings he'd brought and pulling on the gloves before setting off into the house.

The place was a wreck. Old cans of spaghetti-Os and soup were piled up in the kitchen, filling the entire home with a rank, decaying smell. Boone pulled his shirt over his nose and judged Jolene's mom silently. She'd lost her child, so he wanted to give her some leeway here. Nobody could be expected to take good care of themselves after that. Lord knew he wouldn't have. But her daughter had been a psychotic murderer. How much mourning could you reallly do for a kid like that? Or maybe Ms. Dubanik's total lack of housekeeping wasn't a result of Jolene's crazy death. Maybe it was the cause of it? If Dubanik had been a neglectful parent, treating her daughter the way she treated her kitchen, then maybe that explained how Jolene had become radicalized in the first place?

It was what Boone was here to discover.

What had driven Jolene and the others to attack the kids at Camp Tall Pines? And how could Boone stop it from ever happening again? He hoped a neglectful household wasn't the full answer. There was no way he could solve that for every kid in America. But if that was the catalyst, and Boone could figure out what drove them to the next steps...what got them organized...focused...murderous... maybe he could cut that head off the snake.

It took Boone five, maybe ten minutes to find Jolene's room tucked into the very back of the house. Through her window, Boone could see the woods where he'd made his approach, the gap in the fence which he'd slipped through. Jolene's room was surprisingly normal, Boone discovered with a twang of dissatisfaction. He'd expected walls dripping with satanic posters. Pictures of Dahmer and Manson tacked up with creepy hearts drawn around their faces with black lipstick. He'd expected pentagrams carved into the floorboards or candles burned to their bases, maybe even a goat sacrificed in the corner, and all he found were dull beige walls, a stained mattress without any sheets, and a desk cluttered with pens, pencils, and school notebooks.

It all looked so bland and unassuming that for a moment, Boone was certain he'd found the wrong place. But no. There, on the desk, sat a single picture of Jolene herself. She was sitting beside a lake (maybe at Camp Tall PInes?) by herself. She wasn't smiling in the picture, but she wasn't scowling or sneering either, not the way she had been the last time Boone saw her near a lake. Her hair wasn't dripping wet, her clothes weren't blood soaked. In the picture she just looked like a teenager. Gods, she actually looked a decent bit like Athena.

Boone shook his head clear and began picking through the room. He looked through the notebooks on the desk, finding nothing but math homework and timelines about the Revolutionary and Civil Wars with A- and B+ marked at the top in red.

Boone dropped to his hands and knees and glanced under the bed, hoping to find a shoebox filled with cult-ish nonsense tucked away. But no. Nothing but a pair of slippers.

He checked the closet, flipping through the collection of black and grey clothes, the only colors that Jolene wore apparently, but finding nothing. One shirt with a nine-pointed star gave Boone pause, but it was just a band T-Shirt. Slipknot. Nothing overtly demonic.

Boone slumped to the ground and tossed his backpack down beside himself in frustration.

What was he doing here? Was he just some insanely creepy old man, breaking into a teenage girl's room to rummage around. The things that had happened to him at camp. They'd sent him spiraling, hadn't they? Had he lost his mind?

"Well shit."

Was there really nothing here?

Maybe Jolene's mom had gone through and cleaned out all the incriminating evidence about her daughter, but based on the kitchen and the state of the rest of the house, cleaning hardly seemed to be one of Ms Dubanik's strong suits. No, this room was probably in the same state Jolene had left it. So either Jolene was damningly good at cleaning up after herself (possible) or maybe, hopefully, Boone was just missing something.

In a strange way, he missed having the demon in his head. When Shevra had the wheel he'd felt like he had a purpose. A murderous, batshit purpose, but she had sang like sonar in his head, keeping him pointed straight at the enemy at all times. He could have used some of her guidance now. He wondered where she'd gotten off to. When she broke off from him, went traipsing off into the woods, leaving the burning camp behind. Where did she end up?

Boone leaned back, resting his back on the inside of Jolene's closet to close his eyes, give himself a moment to think.

The wall groaned and shifted under his weight and Boone fell backwards, tumbling through the closet, into whatever lay beyond.

Chapter Four

Athena

As the bus pulled up to the school, Athena kept her eyes down on her lap. The freedom high of escaping from home had worn off and her nerves had resurfaced from beneath whatever false confidence had propelled her through her morning. Her hands wouldn't stop shaking. She didn't think she was THAT anxious, but for whatever reason her damned hands just would not stop shaking. The boy in the seat across the aisle from her was doing his best not to stare, but Athena could feel him side-eyeing her, wondering what was wrong with her.

Side-Eyes rose and exited the bus, leaving Athena alone with the bus driver. Athena took a deep breath, raised her eyes, and felt any hope for a normal return to school drain from her in an instant.

The school was a madhouse.

At least four news trucks were parked out front, their reporters and cameramen scattered all across the school's front lawn. A banner had been draped over the front entrance "Welcome back, Athena!" The principal stood at the top of the front steps talking to one of the reporters, gesturing around the school and smiling broadly, playing up whatever publicity stunt this was and trying to cast a positive light on the proceedings. It seemed like the whole student body was outside and, oh shit, was that the band all suited up and waiting for the first glimpse of her?

Athena felt sick.

Why?

Why why why?

Why why why why why?

She sank down in her seat, landing on the sticky, trash-covered floor of the bus, and burying her face in her hands.

Of course it was going to be a circus like this. She was a celebrity now. Her return to school was an event. Everyone wanted to see the hero's return.

There was a knock on the side of the bus. Somebody politely requested to come aboard. Athena peered around the seat and saw the bus driver motion the person up. He threw a thumb backwards towards where Athena was hiding and the whole bus shifted as a new body climbed up the stairs.

Athena took a deep breath and let it out slowly, staring at her damn hand, trying to get it to stop trembling. She imagined a sack of potatoes on top of her. Imagined herself crammed into the back of a pantry in Camp Tall Pines' kitchen, prayed, like she had then, that whoever was coming towards her would pass by her. Maybe then the bus would just drive her back home. This was a mistake. Same as camp had been. She shouldn't have come back out here. Her dad had been right. Again. Shit, how was her dad always right?

"Shit, kid. You know how gross those floors are?"

The voice was deep. Gravelly. Familiar.

Athena looked up and smiled.

Mr. Collier had been an assistant principal at the middle school Athena attended in the 'before times.' He'd dress coded her twice. He'd given her detention for kicking Melanie Spacek during lunch one day when she'd called Athena a stupid slut. But he'd also been the person to find her, bawling her eyes out, when Melanie's words stuck, gained steam, and turned into a school-wide rumor. He'd been the person who actually listened to her. Made her feel safe. Guarded her and watched over her as she walked from class to class in those middle school halls and given her the confidence to finally stand up to Melanie in eighth grade. Right before the Camp Tall Pines Massacre. She had told her off and stood up for herself and NOT kicked at her the second time, and it had all been thanks to Mr. Collier.

He was probably the only person in the world, besides her dad, who she would have been happy to see in the moment.

Mr. Collier reached one of his massive, calloused hands down towards her and lifted Athena off the floor.

"Dust yourself off. Take a second with that makeup if you want to. Can't let the vultures out there see you off your game."

Athena nodded and fished around in her backpack's front pocket for her mirror and eye liner stick. She reapplied her war paint as she asked, in a quiet voice, what Mr. Collier was doing here.

"Got a promotion this summer, kiddo. I got tired of cleaning up idiot middle schoolers' messes. Decided High Schoolers' messes might be more my speed." He winked at Athena. "And girl, you're a mess and a half, aren't you? Taking care of you's probably gonna turn into my full time job, huh? Again?"

Athena smiled awkwardly and nodded.

"I solemnly swear to keep you busy."

"You were always good at that. Keeping me busy."

Athena didn't trust Mr. Collier's fake, slightly exaggerated laid-back attitude. She could tell Mr. Collier wasn't telling her the whole truth. He had always been easy to talk to. Unshakeably 'chill,' but this felt different. Not forced, exactly, but not totally sincere.

Had Mr. Collier been promoted just because of her? The thought flitted through Athena's head, unbidden. He was here on the bus immediately when she pulled up. He was the only person she trusted, and anybody from middle school would have known that. Athena tried to tamp her self-centered paranoia down. Now wasn't the time to look a gift horse in the mouth. Whatever the real reason for his promotion, Athena was glad Collier was here.

She snapped the lid of her mirror closed and poked Mr. Collier in the ribs.

"You're in my way. I've got an appearance to make. My people await."

Mr. Collier chuckled.

"Seriously, kid. Before we go out there. You good? No. Don't answer that. Stupid question. Of course you're not. But when you decide it's all too much, you tell me immediately and I'll get you out of here, okay? No need to be a hero today. Principal Hall knows the deal. We're wading you back into these waters one step at a time."

Athena nodded.

"I'm ready."

"Then let's go face the music."

Chapter Five

Boone

The space Boone fell backwards into was shallow, dusty, and dark. It was only a few feet deep and the top of Boone's head clunked against the back wall of...whatever this space was. The pressure in the air shifted as the darkness all around Boone seemed to inhale, recoiling from its sudden exposure to the sunlight. Nobody was supposed to be here. Least of all, Boone.

It took him a long second to recollect himself and to look around.

A false back to Jolene's closet had given way to a hidden storage compartment that was maybe a foot deep. Jolene, or now Boone, would have to crawl to go into it, but it was perfectly hidden back here behind the dead girl's cluttered wardrobe.

It wasn't too dusty in the secret space. Jolene hadn't been dead *that* long, but the air still tasted stale and empty. As if this was a space that wasn't meant to be visited anymore. Its caretaker had passed on and the hidden compartment had made its peace with never seeing another human face again, settling in for the insects and the bugs from the woodwork to lay their claim. But now, here was Boone, intruding and discovering all its hidden secrets.

Boone sat up, groggy from the blow to his head, and looked around suspiciously. To his right, one of Jolene's yellow wolf masks hung from a nail, glowering down at him and baring its hard plastic fangs. Snarling. Telling him to leave the space alone.

"Let this lie" the mask seemed to growl.

But instead of retreating, Boone smiled.

So there was more to discover here after all.

He wasn't crazy.

Whatever this girl had been up to, this dark space couldn't hide it from him forever. Boone slapped his pockets and pulled out his phone, flicking the flashlight on to illuminate the wolf mask and everything else that lay tucked in the darkness. There was a small box nestled against the back of the space, centered perfectly below the mask with a lock fastened to the front. It was just a simple padlock slapped on a wooden box. He could have gotten through it with his lock pick, given a few minutes of work, but he already felt like he'd been here too long. Jolene's mom shouldn't be back any time soon, but there was no point in testing his luck. Boone would go back to his place, where nobody might accidentally come home early, and three minutes with a jigsaw would get him into the chest.

Better safe than sorry, now that he had what he'd come for.

Boone reached out a gloved hand and picked up the box. The thing was barely larger than a shoebox. Certainly not any heavier. He gave it a quick waggle and felt something thick inside clump around. Maybe a shoe? Or a brick? A book?

Boone grabbed the mask from its nail as well, tossing it on top of the box, then crab-walked his way backwards, out of the closet, and back into the murderous teenager's room. Carefully, Boone replaced the false back to the closet and then, scooping a couple of extra journals and books from Jolene's desk for good measure, Boone made his way back out to his truck.

He followed the same circuitous route he had come in through. He made sure the door was closed and as secure as it could be with that ripped screen. He made sure no neighbors saw him slipping over the fence. He made sure he looked as inconspicuous as possible, wolf mask tucked away in his bag, lock box tucked nonchalantly into his armpit as he walked up the street.

Nobody would know he had been there. Nobody who saw him would have cared. He was just some person out for a casual stroll. Only Jolene's ghost would know what he had really been doing. What he had found. And Boone wasn't afraid of no ghost.

Chapter Six

Athena

"There she is! Our hero! The pride and joy of Bayside."
Principal Hall smiled and threw an arm around Athena, acting like
they were old friends and acquaintances. Pretending like this wasn't
the first time they had seen each other in person, as if somehow being
connected through a brick and mortar building made them kindred
spirits. Athena had looked up some things about the principal online.
He seemed fine. No doubt the Principal had been reading up on her as
well. As the cameras flashed and videographers wormed around,
looking for the perfect shot, Athena and Principal Hall both went
ahead and played up their second-hand knowledge of each other. One
side hug, and a couple quick waves of the hand later, Mr. Collier gave
Principal Hall a look that suggested he know his limits and together the
pair of them ushered Athena into the school, away from the fluttering
lenses. The doors closed behind them, blocking out the sounds of the
reporters calling out interview questions, desperate to justify their trip
out here to their editors.

Inside, Principal Hall dropped the act. He stood up straight,
adjusted his tie, and the smile that had strained his cheeks outside
shrank down to more reasonable proportions. He looked human, not
like the caricature that had been waiting for her to dismount the bus.
Behind her, Athena sensed Mr. Collier relaxing a little bit as well, so
Athena let herself breathe as she adjusted the straps of her backpack.

"So, Ms. Athena Hammond. Welcome to Bayside High School,"
the principal offered with a goofy little shimmy and wave down the

hall. "Now that the vultures outside have been appeased," he said as if he hadn't just been hamming it up for them 30 seconds earlier, "we're going to aim to give you the most normal high school experience possible. This should be a safe space for you to feel like yourself again. Here's your class schedule."

Principal Hall passed her a piece of paper with classes and room numbers printed in neat little rows under the school crest.

"Mr. Collier will help show you the routes between classes. But if anybody gives you a hard time here, I want you to report to me personally. We have a strict no bullying policy."

He said the last part as if any high school ever had been able to control what their student body said or did. Athena nodded along though, pretending to believe the man in an attempt to speed up the conversation so she could get a move on. Shelley was in all three of her first classes and she needed to be reunited with her best friend ASAP.

The principal nodded and glanced down at the paper he'd just handed to her.

"Mr. Csehy for Psychology. He's one of the best. Have fun in there!"

"Sure. Yep. Thanks, Principal Hall," Athena mumbled. She glanced at Collier who led her down the labyrinth of hallways, finally stopping at a seemingly random door and opening it for her. Inside, class was already in session. Mr. Csehy could be heard walking his students through the various sections of the brain, but he was cut short by the ear-piercing screech from the back of the class. Shelley had always been the loud friend in their group, and she held nothing back when she noticed Athena stepping in.

"Good God, I swear, Shelley if you make that noise again I will find a way to fail you in this class," Mr Csehy barked after his initial shock wore off.

Shelley had saved Athena a seat right next to her, and after the awkward initial introductions to the rest of the class (Hi, I'm Athena... she was forced to say despite literally everybody in town knowing who she was now) Athena and Shelley scooted their desks together and passed notes for the next 50 minutes.

What's your next class?

Algebra

Me too!

I know. You texted your schedule to me last night you idiot.

Oh yeah. Duh. Look at you! You look great, babe.

Thanks.

Mr. Csehy saw the notes getting passed back and forth, but chose not to address it. As long as there wasn't a cell phone out, it seemed like he would pick his battles.

Maybe the other kids were nervous to bother Athena. Maybe there had been some big assembly where Principal Hall threatened the student body not to harass Athena when she returned. Maybe Mr. Csehy just ruled his classroom with an iron fist. Whatever the reason was, everything went so smoothly through her first, second, even third classes that Athena felt herself slipping into a cool, calm, collected routine. It was nice.

But then there was lunch.

The second that the teachers and administrators were relegated to the sidelines, the vultures descended. Athena barely had time to put her tray down before some rando who she hadn't ever met before swung by the table.

"Glad you're okay, Athena! We all missed you."

Athena looked around, to see if anybody else nearby was named Athena.

"Umm...thanks?"

The stranger hung around for a second longer, seeming like she wanted to keep talking, but Shelley arrived with Marco in tow, sitting next to Athena and scaring away the rando with a sharp glance. But the first well wisher was followed by another, and another, and another.

"Glad you're back."

"Are you okay?"

"That must have been so scary! I'm glad you're okay."

Athena tried to remain polite, nodding to everybody and mumbling "Thank you"s between bites of food.

"You're so brave. Like, I never could have... Like. Oh my gosh. Just so brave."

"Yo, chick. Badass way to survive that. Want my number?"

"Run, little lamb. Run."

The last one came in Jolene's voice, the whisper cutting through the crowd like a scythe through campers. The hair on Athena's neck leapt to attention and she white knuckled her little plastic knife, scanning the room only to decide the voice was only in her head.

The crowd around their table was getting bigger, with seemingly every Bayside student lining up to say their piece to the most famous girl on campus. Like this was some table signing at a comic convention or something, the popularity leeches were swarming. Simon and Meredith muscled their way through the crowd, elbows and shoulders flying to defend their trays of food. They slid into the last two seats beside Shelley and Marco, and it took Athena an extra minute to place the pair of them.

Meredith had cut her hair since middle school, dropping her trademark bangs for more of a punky pixie cut. She was smart. Calculated. The reluctant, defacto leader in every group project Athena had worked with her on. One of those types. She didn't take the lead on things to start with. She didn't like being the center of attention. But invariably, once everybody else had proven their incompetence, Meredith would take the helm to save them all.

Simon had let his hair grow out and wore horn-rimmed glasses now in some sort of a hipster anti-stylish fashion statement. Quiet, reserved, Simon was a kid who intentionally never led a group project. To do that would draw way too much attention to himself when all he wanted to do was melt into the fantasy novel he was reading.

Athena had known both of them in middle school. They were peripheral members of the hangout group, like Marco. Not core members like Athena, or Shelley, or-

"- Elena" Jolene's voice whispered again, and this time Athena crossed her arms over her chest, dropping her eyes and trying to hide the tears welling up inside her. Shelley noticed the reaction and stood up, planting both feet on her chair and rising a foot over the crowd.

"Look, assholes!"

"Language!" a teacher yelled from the back.

"You all need to back off. Give my girl some space. You want to say hi? You want to tout around some false connection to a girl you all blew off in Middle School? Well not like this. You crowd her again and I'll make sure they have to wire all your jaws shut so tight you can't even frappe your pizza enough to get it past your teeth. Capiche?"

"No threats!" the same teacher yelled, but none of the adults moved to help alleviate the situation. They seemed to think Shelley had it covered.

"Hypocrites. We remember how much you bullied us a year ago. And yeah, Athena's famous now, but it's because she had a traumatic experience, you insensitive pricks! That doesn't mean she's got fucking-"

"Language"

"-amnesia. Melanie Spacek? Speak of the devil herself, what are *you* doing in this line? Get out. Go back to your lunches. Act normal, you fame pervs."

Shelley's speech had its intended effect, and the crowd dissolved, most of the students walking back to their usual tables, deflated, their empty claims of camaraderie dying on their lips.

Athena went through the breathing exercises her therapist had taught her. Long, slow breaths. Go back to her happy place. The fictional summer camp where the counselors weren't trying to kill her. The fictional summer camp where Elena was still alive, winning canoe races alongside Athena and the rest of their cabin. The fictional summer camp that Athena had begged her dad to take her to, in the before-times.

Mr. Collier appeared in the middle of the crowd like a jump scare, watching the other students intently, making sure nobody tried anything funny. Had he been there the whole time? Making sure things didn't get out of hand? Athena latched onto the sight of him like a lifeline, finding her center before any tears had a chance to escape. That was good. She didn't want anybody here to think she was weak. Nobody could see her cry. She nodded at Mr. Collier, giving him the all-clear, and Collier winked at her before turning back to rejoin the teacher's table.

The rest of lunch was uncomfortable, with Shelley and Marco carrying most of the conversation, Meredith and Simon chiming in occasionally, and Athena just trying, unsuccessfully, to get into the same headspace she had started the day with. She was back at school. She was surrounded by people. She should be happy. This was normal.

Except it wasn't.

Despite the three classes of "normal" that Athena had managed, the whispers around her in the cafeteria revealed the true story. Normal was dead. Dead like Elena. Dead like Jolene. On the surface, school looked like everything Athena had hoped for, but it was just a mask. A thin veil her peers wore so they could get along easily. Just below the surface, Camp Tall Pines followed her. Waited for its chance to strike. As soon as the teachers turned their backs, it would resurface again. Through the questions the other students asked. Through the glances they threw at her when they thought she wasn't looking. She was still surrounded by wolves in sheep's clothing. Just now the weapons wouldn't be scythes, spears, or goddamn chainsaws. Now the weapons would be false sincerity. Fake friends. Goddamn *pity*.

Welcome to High School, Athena thought to herself as her lunch went untouched in front of her.

Chapter Seven
Marco

That night, as Athena and Boone sat at their dinner table, Athena talking about her day, Boone lying about his, Marco found himself still stuck at Bayside High's Sweetwater Stadium. Marco was a kicker for the football team, and so he'd been made to stay extra late. Somehow when their quarterback missed a wide open receiver, losing Bayside the game last Friday, to the coaches that meant that the kicker had to stay late also. Their practice had been a backbreaker, with the whole team suffering for their quarterback's shortcomings. A three hour practice in full pads concluded with everybody running laps until Timmy Claypool peeled off to the sidelines and threw up all over an assistant coach's shirt. The coaches had finally let the team go shower, but it was too late for Marco. His mom was already off to work. His dad so drunk that he wasn't answering his phone, probably passed out on the couch. Marco had missed his window to get a ride home.

So he sat down in the cold, hard bleachers, weighing his options.

He could walk home. It was a half hour slog if he cut through the woods and climbed a couple fences.

Or he could call Shelley. She'd bailed him out countless times before. Surely she'd bail him out again. He thumbed his phone open, found Shelley's picture in his recent contacts, and his bestie answered before the third ring.

"Again?" Shelley said by way of greeting.

"Again," Marco confirmed.

"One of these days you're gonna have to pay me back for all this gas. Between the school, the library, and rehearsals, I figure I've got an entire 401k worth of backpay waiting for me.

Marco rolled his eyes, but Shelley was right. He relied on her way too much. Even so, he heard the jangle of car keys through the phone's speaker.

"On my way, dingus."

"Thanks."

"Hey. Wanna talk about today?"

"Yeah. Actually. Crazy seeing Athena waltzing into school like that, huh?"

There was some movement down, at the end of the bleachers. Like somebody, or something, slipping down, through the slats between the seats. Surely it was just a trick of the moonlight, but Marco stood up anyhow, using his shoulder to pin his phone to his ear as he gathered his backpack and gym bag. He kept a curious eye trained on the dark slats between the stadium steps as he stood, trying to stay focused on what Shelley was saying.

"Yeah. There were a few moments where I thought she was about to panic, but she managed to stay pretty cool. Tomorrow's bound to be a different story though. The teachers can't keep the student body sedated forever. The judgment armistice will fall, D-Day will come, and Athena's going to need us to lean on."

"Right. And we need to hold off talking to her about Camp Tall Pines, right?"

"Obviously. Did you see how she shut down at lunch when everyone else crowded her? We're supposed to be her friends. No massacre talk. Not yet. Not until she feels more comfortable."

"Roger that, boss."

Shelley chuckled. Marco chuckled. Something under the bleachers chuckled.

Every hair on Marco's neck shot up at the sound. So somebody was there after all.

"Hey, um…Shell? I think I'm gonna have to call you back. There's somebody here."

"Coach?"

"Nah. It's… I dunno. I'll see you in a few though. We can keep working on the Athena situation in the car."

"Coolio. Don't get a ride with anyone else. I'll be there in a tick. If I drive all the way back to the school for nothing, I'm gonna be pissed."

Marco hurdled the side of the bleachers, creating some distance from whoever was screwing with him from under the steps. The Field House was just a few steps away. He could duck in there, throw the lights on, and wait until he heard Shelley pull up. He glanced back just once, as he slid into the building. There was somebody beneath the bleachers all right. But Marco didn't slow down enough to see who it was. He didn't care. Some goth creep most likely. But just to be safe, Marco slid a trash can in front of the door, forming a sort of metallic alarm system. If Bleacher Creep followed him in here, he'd knock over the trash can and Marco would hear him coming.

Backpedalling, his eyes trained on the door as he retreated, Marco made his way back to the gym. He sat down on the seat for the bench press and opened his bag. Dirty clothes and homework that he didn't want to do stared back at him, but he knew that somewhere deep down, near the bottom, was a granola bar. He plunged his hand into the dank, fragrant chaos just as the lights snapped off around him.

Pitch black smothered him like a blanket, and even the emergency light over head, usually so watchful, so consistent, hid its face, refusing to watch what was about to happen.

"Mother…"

Marco withdrew his hand from his bag and fumbled around in his pocket, looking for his phone's flashlight.

There was a bang to his left in the darkness. Something heavy crash landing on the gym's weightlifting mats. Like Donny had just finished a power cling except Donny wasn't here. Was he?

"Aaaaaah shit."

Marco freed the phone from his pants, flicked on the flashlight, and saw a trash can sitting in the middle of everything. Had that been there before? Or was that the one he had put in front of the-

The 45 lb barbell arced through the darkness, landing center-mass on Marco like a baseball bat and caving in his chest with a single blow. Marco spun backwards, head cracking against the pull-up station behind him. He was dead before he ever hit the ground.

But that didn't stop his attacker from carrying on.

Shelley pulled up in front of the Field House ten minutes later. She honked her horn once, twice, thrice in frustration, then cursed Marco' name and drove back home. That asshole must have gotten a ride with somebody else. Melanie Gibson or Brock Howard or some other footballer or cheerleader that had stayed late. At least Marco should have had the decency to call Shelley, to cancel on her.

She was gonna give him hell when she saw him tomorrow. And she was never going to come pick him up after practice again. He'd blown her off one time too many.

Chapter Eight

Boone

"I told you there was more to find," Boone said excitedly, the tape recorder spinning back up.

"And I told you not to look for anything else," Doctor Carver responded. "It didn't matter if there was more to find or not. That's all external. What we're working on here is internal growth. Acceptance. And moving on."

"But don't you see? It might not be over yet. And I couldn't move on before since there was this itch in my mind. This instinct that danger was still out there. And maybe I was right. If I can just follow this lead. Pull on this thread. Maybe..."

"...Maybe the whole sweater comes unraveled. I think there's a Weezer song about it or something."

"You aren't taking this seriously, doc."

"On the contrary, I'm taking it very seriously. You've latched onto this potential danger. I believe the technical phrase for it is hypervigilance. These threats from the shadows that you can't even give form or function to, you're just convincing yourself that they still exist. It's a common reaction to trauma that makes everything seems dangerous. Sometimes it's right. Sometimes it's wrong. But you will have to teach yourself how to sort one from the other again."

"Shadows tend to stem from real, tangible things, doc. If I can see shadows, but not the threat, it just means the threat is standing right behind me."

We hear the sound of Doctor Carver blowing air through her nose in frustration.

"Fine. The matter of speech got away from me. But Boone, if you lose yourself to this, keep turning over rocks like you are, then there's the chance you'll draw even more attention to yourself. You could wake up whatever threat is lying dormant. Not saying there is a threat, but...ugh... Now you have me going down your logical rabbit hole."

"Listen, doc. I might stop seeing you for a bit."

"I would advise against that."

"I know your job is to get me to put the past behind me. I can appreciate that. But I really don't think this is over yet. I've gotta see it through, then once things are settled, I'll come get the help I need."

"I think that's a mistake."

"I know you do, doc."

"But it's your mistake to make. I'm not here to command you around or anything. That's not supposed to be my job. I give you all the advice that I want, but you still have to make your own decisions. And if THIS is your decision, then I want to help you find the best way through it all. The last thing I'd want is for you to get hurt."

"Thanks, doc."

"But one last question before you go."

"Shoot."

"Where does it end? What's the point that you'll look around and decide that things are 'settled' as you put it? Do you even know what that would look like?"

There's the scrape of a chair as Boone stands up to leave.

"I don't. But I'll tell you all about it when I find out."

Chapter Nine

Athena

By the time Athena woke up the next morning, the circus had already arrived. Blue lights flashed from the other side of her curtains, and cries of 'Get Back' and 'Care to Comment?' polluted the air in the place of the song birds. On her night stand, her phone glowed and vibrated constantly, its screen never fading to black, the buzzing never stopping because another text would come in, then another, then another, keeping the phone active, awake, screaming for Athena to pick it up, to save it from the deluge of messages it was receiving. Athena sat on the end of her bed, knees hugged up to her chest, crying freely into the pillow she clutched.

Marco.

She hadn't read many of the texts when she woke up. Just the one from Shelley. But that was enough. A janitor had found his body that morning, speared upright on the football tackling sled like one of the team's practice dummies.

They were back. Those damned cultists were back.

From the yard, Athena heard her dad yelling something about restraining orders and lawsuits, but it didn't sound like the vultures with the press badges cared about his idle threats.

Tears slid down Athena's face as she white-knuckled her phone. Pictures of her dead friend had leaked already. She knew because text after text from unknown numbers had picture attachments that Athena knew, *knew* she shouldn't look at. But her thumbs had minds of their own, and scabs from old traumas are far too easy to pick at.

The bones in Marco's arms and legs looked like they had been shattered. They hung by his sides like streamers, bending in all the wrong places. One of the vertical shafts from the football sled had been jammed up him, through a gash in his pants, holding Marcus's body impaled, upright, like...like...

Like the first Cultist at the bonfire

She didn't want to acknowledge it. She was so stupid for thinking that she could have friends. That she could return to a normal life and there would be no consequences. No ghosts from Tall Pines to follow her home. Haunt her wherever she went. Her dad had killed all of those bastards back at the camp, but she should have known that wouldn't be the end of it. Somehow, some way, somebody knew what happened there. And now they were, what? Coming to get revenge on her? On her dad? Making an example of her friends by massacring Marco?Seeing Marco, her friend, destroyed and served up to the Reaper the same way that cultist from camp had been added an insult to injury that Athena wasn't ready to grapple with.

The door to Athena's room opened, slowly.

Outside, her dad kept shouting at reporters to leave their family the hell alone.

A shadow filled the doorway, watched Athena as she sobbed, for a short moment, then rushing in to tackle her.

Athena yelped. Cocked her fist back to defend herself.

But it was Shelley.

"Girl, they are *everywhere* outside. I had to walk like, a mile, through the creek to sneak up to your back door. And even then I'm pretty sure one of the cops saw me and just turned the other cheek. House arrest round two?"

"Looks like it." Athena wiped her tears away with the back of her hand, trying to put on a brave face. She hugged Shelley, pulling her friend closer and closer until she heard her back pop. Shelley didn't pull away. Instead she just hugged Athena back, burying her face in her friends' hair.

"I'm so sorry about this."

"Shut up, bitch. You know it's not your fault."

Athena didn't argue. She didn't have to. They both knew Shelley was just trying to make her feel better. The hollow excuse of unintention failing to actually absolve Athena of anything. Maybe she didn't *mean to* bring a pack of killers back home with her. But it had happened anyway. Marco was dead, and if Athena hadn't come home, he would still be alive. Causation. Correlation. Check, check, check.

They sat on Athena's floor, wordlessly embracing, for what seemed like hours, until Shelley finally forced Athena to rise and to go find some breakfast.

Two eggs and some coffee helped to reset Athena's mind. She asked how everybody else from the friends group was doing.

"Not so sure. You were my first thought, and everybody else has texted, but not much. Mostly it just sounds like they're sad."

"Oh."

"Simon literally just texted back 'wtf,' but Meredith sent me this 10 million character novel of a text talking about how insane it was. She had just been talking to him yesterday and now she'd never see him again. What'd they say to you?"

Athena shrugged and glanced at her phone. She'd put it on silent mode so that the constant bing-ing and buzz-ing wouldn't drive her totally insane. Her unread messages had reached the triple digits by that point, and Athena thumbed the device open to try to wade into the madness.

The first ten or so messages were from unknown numbers. Reporters, likely the same ones that were outside now, asking for interviews. Asking if she knew anything before the news had even broke.

Then there was Mr. Collier's number. Still saved in her phone from Middle School. "So sorry, kiddo. Let me know if you need help." Short. Simple. Direct. Mr. Collier really was the best.

Reporters. Reporters. Melanie Gibson, the bully, texting to pretend like she and Athena were friends, but working her little jabs in as always. '...I know you didn't *mean to* get Marco killed, but I'm just so sorry..."

The bitch.

Then there was Meredith, like Shelley said, with an absolute door stopper of a text message. It all sounded sincere. Heartfelt. The girl was gonna need therapy. Fortunately, Athena knew a few good ones.

Simon had texted 'You Good?' Shelley, reading over Athena's shoulder, laughed and Athena was about to reply something snarky back when the front door swung open.

Her dad reentered the home, fuming, escorted by two other men and shouting something backwards over his shoulder.

"Keep them off my damn lawn. If I see any of them peeking through my windows, I'm going to break them."

Athena shuddered, remembering her dad, tentacles tearing through his skin, standing in the middle of an ablaze Camp Tall Pines. Most of that had been the demon, she knew. But still. Idle threats didn't feel so idle coming from her dad anymore. Not when she'd seen him -or at least an extension of him- bisecting cultists with a freaking chainsaw.

She glanced at Shelley to see if her dad's shouting and threats had rattled her friend, but she seemed fine.

The cops on either side of Boone jumped to attention at the sight of the girls. Apparently they hadn't expected them to be in the kitchen.

"Who are you?"

"Shelley"

"How did you get in here?"

"Magic" and Shelley waggled her fingers in the air with all the sarcastic gusto that defined overconfident high schoolers.

Behind them, the door opened and closed again. A man in a black button-down, smooth-pressed khakis, and polished black shoes stepped into the Hammond house.

"Um...hello?" Boone asked.

The man pulled off his shades and pulled out a badge.

"Detective Ramsey. FBI."

"Shit. You guys again?"

"Us guys again."

As if the morning hadn't had enough drama already.

"I think we should head upstairs," Athena whispered, but Detective Ramsey heard her and stared down his nose, locking his cold, hard gaze on her.

"I think you should stay right where you are. In case you weren't aware, based on the number of reporters in your yard, and the number of police in your house, there was a murder last night. And based on your, and your father's history? I'd like to keep suspects number one and number two where I can see them. At least until we have a little talk."

"Lawyer."

"Yeah. I'm gonna go ahead and go," Shelley said, standing.

"Not before you give your name and information to Officer…" Ramsey leaned forward, checked the name on the badge of the officer beside him. "…Cyrill over here."

Shelley's mouth flopped open and shut, her eyes darting from Athena, to Boone, to the officers. The poor girl. She'd never been confronted by the police before. This was old hat for the Hammonds by now, but Shelley looked like she was about to break down in tears again.

"Jesus, let the girl go and we'll talk to you, Detective. Don't freak out the poor high schooler."

Ramsey's eyes touched base on each of the civilians in the kitchen one at a time.

"Fine. Tell him your name then get going."

Shelley nodded and slipped from the stool where she'd been sitting, approaching the officer as Boone led the Detective and Athena into the living room.

"You not gonna offer me coffee or anything?" Ramsey asked with a smirk on his face.

"Not after that entrance, no." Boone said. But Athena walked slowly through the kitchen, grabbed a mug and started filling it for the detective.

It bought her an extra minute to think.

This was not good. The Marco stuff, obviously, but now the presence of Detective Ramsey threatened to send everything about Athena's 'return to normalcy' down the shitter. He was the detective that had been the hard ass back at Camp Tall Pines. While everybody else involved in the investigation had been busy offering Boone and Athena towels and medical attention and taking care of them, Detcctive Ramsey seemed to have a sixth sense that something else was afoot. Boone and Athena played the part of the victim. Because honestly, truthfully, they WERE the victims. But there was more to their story than JUST being the victims. Wasn't there? Ramsey seemed like the one person to pick up on that. A dog with a scent, and he wouldn't let it go, through any of their interviews. Now here he was in their home.

Athena filled the cup and skipped the cream and the sugar on assumption. She went into the living room where Detective Ramsey had seated himself in a chair, oriented so that he could still see her back in the kitchen. He never took his eyes off her.

She offered him the mug and he eyed the 'LIVE LAUGH LOVE' on the side with disdain.

"Where were you all last night?"

"In bed. Doing homework. My first day of school was yesterday."

"Uh-huh. You?"

"In the basement. Working."

"You're fighting fires in your basement now? I'd love to hear how that work from home situation plays."

"I'm finishing the basement. Building a panic room."

The detective stopped and raised his eyes towards Boone in something like amusement.

"Really?"

"Really."

"Hah. Well that seems appropriate, given the circumstances. I don't suppose anybody could vouch for your whereabouts though? A neighbor that came over to drop off a freshly baked pie. Actually saw you here after sundown? Nothing like that?"

"Nope. Truck was in the driveway all night though. Maybe you could ask a neighbor to verify that."

"I intend to."

"And how about the kid that died. What's your connection to him?"

"He's my friend from school." Athena said.

"So you know who the victim was?"

"It was Marco. The press leaked his name hours ago and it's all over my text messages. Don't act like you caught me in something."

"Athena, calm down," Boone said the words plainly, without really meaning them.

"I can't believe the Detective can just show up here and accuse us of having anything to do with this. There's no connection to us besides 'somebody dying' and with no evidence at all, here we are getting interrogated. It's bullshit," Athena spat the words, tears leaking from her eyes.

"Athena!" Boone scolded.

But the detective just smiled.

"Oh! The picture leaked to the press, huh? Look at that picture again, Athena. See how close the cameraman was when they took the picture? How there isn't a single person investigating the crime scene? Almost like all the police, detectives, and coroners were asked to take a biiiiig step back while somebody staged the photograph. How do you think the media got that close with police tape already strung up everywhere?"

He waited a minute. Let Athena flip her phone back open, look at the disfigured photo of her dead friend.

"It's not exactly standard protocol. But I like the move. You collect a bit of evidence, a couple of details, that nobody else knows about, and you keep those pieces of evidence hidden away. Make sure nobody can come out of the woodwork to claim to be the killer, unless they know what the missing pieces are. There's some sickos and weirdos out there, Hammonds. Mark my words. Sickos and weirdos who want the credit for a catastrophe like this. They want the fame. So they'll see a picture like that one on your phone, and they'll call the police station, and they'll say they did it. "Put me in the spotlight, pigs.""

But any posers wont be able to answer questions about the missing piece. The thing we hid. So we'll know they're a fraud."

"So what's the missing piece?" Boone asked.

Detective smiled cruelly at Athena's dad. He tapped his nose with a finger and winked, as if the two of them shared a secret.

"Next question," Detective Ramsey said as he reached into the small bag that he had with him. He undid the zipper and pulled out an evidence bag with something large, bulky, and yellow inside.

"And I want straight, clear answers to this question. No more attitude. We're all gonna play nice or we're all gonna go to the station together. Finish this talk from behind bars."

He spun the evidence bag around and pressed the plastic down around the wolf mask. The same mask that the killers from Camp Tall Pines had worn. VERMIN had been carved across the forehead of the mask and the left side was stained with Marco's dried blood.

"So what the fuck is *this thing* doing in Bayside?"

Athena looked, horrified, towards her dad. Hell really had followed them home.

Chapter Ten

Detective Ramsey

Detective Ramsey stayed at Boone and Athena's house for more than five hours. By the time he left, Boone felt fairly confident that he'd convinced the man that neither he, nor his daughter, had anything to do with the high school kids' murder. But it was a damnable exercise, proving that you had spent a night at home alone. Athena had ordered a movie online at 10 o'clock and the Fast and the Furious receipt seemed to validate her alibi in the eyes of the detective. But Boone didn't have any such exculpatory time stamps laying around.

"Where were you?"

"In the basement."

Variations of that question and answer had been batted back and forth, back and forth, like some redundant game of verbal ping-pong, all culminating in a huff and Detective Ramsey asking if there was anything the Hammonds knew that could help move the investigation along. Was there anything they 'suddenly remembered' from camp that could help them figure out who the masked killer was. He promised not to hold them in contempt for 'forgetting' to tell him earlier.

It was a desperate plea. Boone had seen the yearning in the Detective's eyes for just one more piece of evidence. He wanted, maybe needed, to know what he had missed at camp.

Boone thought about the cardboard box, filled with information about the killers from camp hidden in his basement. He thought about

Jolene's mask and the locked box he had found in her hide-space, now tucked away next to the profiles of all the other psychopaths.

He still hadn't broken into that box yet. For a split second, he tried to figure out how he could use it to throw Ramsey a bone. "Look what I found. It's not even open yet. I wonder what's inside." Pass the burden of the blame along to the Detective. Get one small, tiny thing like breaking and entering, withholding evidence off his conscience.

But there was no way he could show anything downstairs to the Detective. In Ramsey's eyes, possession of any sort of evidence would just confirm to him that Boone was the killer.

Maybe he didn't have to hand him anything though. Maybe he could tell the Detective about Shevra. That demon was still out there somewhere, wasn't she? He'd seen her separate from him. Saw her go dancing off into the flames of camp, and she was bound to be watching over all of this somewhere, somehow, wasn't she? And that wasn't a crime, right? Being possessed by a Demon? As long as Boone didn't explain the connection between the Demon and the murders, maybe he could pass all the blame for them along to his parasite.

But no. The Detective would just dismiss all that as supernatural bullshit. Bring Boone in on an insanity charge.

So, Boone kept his damn mouth shut. How could he protect Athena from behind bars?

When Ramsey finally left, he told the Hammonds that the police would be stationed outside until the whole thing wrapped up. The Hammonds were free to come and go as they pleased. They couldn't arrest them without evidence. But they wouldn't let anybody in, or out, without checking them out.

Boone watched the man leave through a gap in the front blinds. The press was all over the place out there, but like Ramsey had promised, a few local police had erected a small barricade on the street, keeping the Press the legally required distance away from a residence. Plastic sawhorses lined the road, and Boone saw his neighbor, Mrs. Rogers, struggling to get to her driveway.

There would be no leaving the house today. But that was fine. He had work to do in the basement anyhow. Could find some way to keep himself busy. And there were Jolene's books and journals. He had some reading to do.

"You okay, sweetie?" he asked Athena, still crumpled on the couch.

"Yeah. No. I dunno, Dad. Is...is all this our fault?"

Boone saw the tears in his daughter's eyes. The hurt and the shame contained therein. He abandoned his thoughts of Jolene in an instant, dropped to the couch beside his daughter instead.

"Of course not." He tried to think back to all his sessions with Doctor Carver. All the ways she'd tried to counsel him through his own guilt. It hadn't worked for him. But maybe for Athena here...

"You can't control what other people do. You can only control how you react to it. You're a good person, Athena. Back at that camp, we did what we had to do to survive. And even in the middle of that nightmare, you were still trying to help people. This cult following us home? That's on them. That's all on them. And you know what? I'm not even scared of them this time."

Athena cocked an eyebrow at that.

"Because we're together this time. At camp that was my biggest fear. What if I had lost you? But here? Now? With you by my side? Whatever these assholes have planned, they don't stand a chance."

Boone raised a fist for Athena to bump.

"Those idiots show up at our door, we're gonna bust some faces."

Athena rolled her eyes at the old saying, but she bumped the fist.

"We need a new catch phrase."

"I dunno. The classic has been working well enough so far. You don't pull a pitcher in the middle of a perfect game."

"I don't understand baseball references, dad."

"I know, sweetie. I'm not going to let anything happen to you. Not again. I want you to just focus on getting your life back to normal. Hang out with friends. Do well in school. You worry about normal teenager stuff and let me worry about protecting you. I'm a dad. That's my job."

Athena nodded, slowly.

"Wanna watch Zombies Vs Ninjas? Get some ideas for how to knock these cultists on their asses?" Boone suggested.

"We need to invest in katanas."

"And grenades."

"Can we please get landmines?"

The two of them laughed and hugged, laying together on the couch for a long minute before Athena finally pulled herself free from her father's bear hug and found the remote. They ended up steering clear of the bloody movie, opting instead for a few rounds of Mario Kart. Blue shells and banana peels wouldn't accidentally trigger either of their memories of the massacre. Koopas and Yoshis were safe. They zipped in circles, round and round the Rainbow Road until the bright light of day faded to darkness, punctuated by the flash of the barricade of blue lights standing guard outside.

Chapter Eleven

Athena

Athena didn't remember how long she and her dad played their games, but she looked over in the middle of a character select screen and saw her dad slumped to the side, mouth ajar, a light snore building up steam in his lungs. She pulled a blanket over him gently and went upstairs to tuck herself into her bed. She lay in the dark, sliding easily into sleep, and failed to hear her window slide open. Failed to see the figure dressed all in black come slipping in, soundlessly, like a cat.

When the intruder's hand clamped over Athena's mouth, disorientation caused her fear to spike. She thrashed out, swinging her arm at her assailant, hoping to connect with flesh, organs, bone, anything that could do some damage, praying to get nails-full of something that could buy her an advantage in the struggle. But she whiffed. Missed her attacker completely and instead punched the shit out of her nightstand.

Pain flared up in her knuckles and she screamed into the soft leather gloves that her attacker wore.

"Shut up, bitch! Jaysus."

Shelley's voice. Athena stopped flailing about and focused, finding her intruder's face and recognizing her friend's eyes behind the ski mask.

"Calm down. There ya go. Okay fine, that's on me. I shouldn't have snuck in like that. Not with everything that's going on. But, you know, the police are watching your front door like a bunch of assholes and they wouldn't have let me through, so I went with the classic window entry, and then you were just lying there so peacefully...I had to screw with you, and-"

"-What are you doing here?"

"I'm busting you out. You had one day free from quarantine and now they're slamming you back into house arrest? Nuh-uh. Not on my watch. You've earned your freedom, little birdie. Parole for good behavior, that's my verdict. Now come on, the others are waiting. We're going bowling or something. You can choose. Doesn't matter."

"I'm supposed to stay here."

"Are you serious? I saw how happy you were at school. Don't tell me you don't miss the outside world. It's just us. The friends group. We've got your back, okay?"

Athena lay still one more second, her blanket and comforter hugging her close, begging her not to go. But Shelley was right. Those stupid cultists had taken enough of her life from her already. They didn't get a single night more.

She replaced her sweatpants with jeans, pulled on some socks and shoes, then followed Shelley out her own window. The night was pleasantly cool, and the rustling of the leaves as Athena and Shelley climbed down the tree, into her back yard, helped to drown out the sounds of police and press chatter from the front lawn. As the leaves scritched and scratched, it was almost possible to forget the horrors of the world. To just exist as two carefree kids climbing a tree in the back yard. Athena lost herself in the moment. How many times had she and Elena monkeyed around in this tree? Hanging upside down, letting their hair go wild, snagging in the branches. Even Marco, who Athena hadn't been best friends with, had climbed the tree with her before, when the kids had entertained designs of a tree house with a trap door and real, working windows, and a slide into a pool full of Jell-O.

"Hey, Elena. I..."

Athena's heart sank. Elena was dead.

"What's that, Athena?" Shelley called back over her shoulder.

But Athena didn't want to acknowledge the slip she'd made. She landed on the ground and followed Shelley, quietly, to the spot in her back fence where the creek curved below the boards, giving the kids enough room to squeeze underneath, assuming they didn't mind getting a little wet.

"So, what are we doing? Bowling sounds so lame when I say it out loud, but there's not MUCH else to do this late at night. We could go to the movies, but there's not much showing besides that horror movie, and..." Shelley didn't say it out loud.

"Movie. Let's go see a movie."

"But, girl. It's a slasher. Dead bodies and- "

"I can handle it."

"Never mind. I shouldn't have even suggested it. You've been stuck in your house watching movies for months. You want to do something active, don't you?"

"Movie theater popcorn. I want movie theater popcorn, and I want to sit in the back row of a theater, and I want to make jokes about bad actors being bad actors with my friends."

Shelley stared at her, distrusting, for just a moment.

Athena stared back, unflinching, a brave face plastered on. Did she really want to go see the movie? Not really. She loved horror movies. Always had. Her tolerance was low for jump scares, but she enjoyed the thrill of them all the same. It had always been her and her dad's thing, watching zombie movies, cheering for the characters as they dismembered their foes. The outside world didn't get to take that from her. It had taken too much already.

"Alright. Cool. I'll text the others, let them know about the pivot. And seriously, bitch, if we get there and it's too much, you just say the word and we'll go bowling. No need to fake it around us. We know you're a badass already."

Shelley gave Athena a big, heartfelt hug, and together they wound their way through the maze of back yards that led towards the strip. Picket fences were scaled. Children's playsets were scaled and slid down. Pools, covered in preparation for the cold months, were circumvented safely. And all the while, Athena and Shelley talked, and giggled, and laughed, and fell back into old form. All their side jokes were still funny. All their memories from middle school were still cherished. And when their thoughts turned to Elena or Marco, there was love there. Sadness at the loss of their friend, sure, but sharing the longing with another person helped dull the pain enough for Athena to remember the love that had been there. Allowed her to think about the good times without the sting of the bad being so all-consuming. It turned out that friendship was good medicine.

They made it to the theater just as the credits started, took their time to get popcorn for Athena, then found the rest of their friends in the back row, exactly like Athena had hoped for.

It should have been a perfect night. It should have been exactly what Shelley had pitched. It should have been healing and laughter and youth bonding.

It wasn't.

Chapter Twelve

Boone

"Boone. Do you realize what time it is?"

"Sorry, Doc. Crazy day. I Need to talk."

"Seriously. We have a calendar for a reason. You're supposed to schedule these meetings."

"I know. I know. I know. It's just… It happened again."

"What happened again? You ignored me and did the opposite of what we talked about?"

"No. There was another killing."

"Right."

"A kid from Athena's school. Marco."

"And you think it's connected to the incident at the camp?"

"They found a mask with the body. Same wolf mask. Same brutality. Doc, the cult came home with us."

There's a long pause as the tape recorder crackles thoughtfully.

"Well. Have you looked through the box from Jolene's place like you planned to?"

"Not yet. I haven't had time."

"Remember when I told you to forget about all of this? To put it all behind you and to try to rebuild your life? Move on and enter Phase 2?"

"Of course. And I'm trying, Doc, but there's no way I can look past this. Things clearly aren't settled, and I can't just turn a blind eye to-"

"-You're right."

"I'm what?"

A beat, as the therapist takes a long, frustrated breath. "I was, apparently, wrong. You were right. Listen, there's a difference between needing to move on from a resolved situation and needing help navigating an ongoing conflict. Now, I'll admit, I might not have been the best therapist for you with post-trauma healing. It didn't feel like we were getting anywhere. Maybe once everything wraps up this time, I'll help you find a different specialist in the field."

"Are you serious?"

"As the grave, Mr. Hammond. But if you're right, and if these Cultist freaks followed you home, then I need you to start really listening to me. I want to help you through this, but you have to recognize how emotionally invested you have become in these events. You cannot allow anger and frustrations to drive your obsession. Your fears about your daughter are clouding your judgment. If you keep bull-charging through your problems, you're going to break something you aren't intending to. Maybe it'll be your own mental health that breaks. Maybe it will be the people you love. But you have to slow down and let people help. Let me help. Open up to me and let me guide you again."

There is another long pause as the tape recorder crackles along. You can practically hear Boone weighing his options through the audio.

"Tell me more about the Marco kid," Dr. Carver says at last, her tone softer again.

"Yeah. Alright."

Chapter Thirteen

Athena

Athena burst out the front doors of the theater in a panic, trying to get away. The air is brisk and thin. Behind her, Shelley, Meredith, and Simon were right on her heels and, try as she might, Athena just couldn't get any space from them. She doubled over at the waist, clutched her stomach, and vomited all over the sidewalk, in full view of all her friends.

"Ew. Shit." Meredith said behind Athena, sounding just as disgusted as Athena had feared.

Athena tried to control her stomach, but those images from the screen stuck with her. She hadn't even made it through the opening salvo of kills. The first wave of teenagers, camping in the woods. The ones who you knew were doomed from the start. Necessary sacrifices to establish the killer. At the first crunch of bone and splash of blood, Athena's head had spun. It all looked so fake. CGI bullshit played across the screen in a pathetic excuse for artistry. But somehow it had worked on Athena. Thinking about how fake that blood looked had reminded Athena of the real sights, sounds, and smells surrounding a massacre. She couldn't handle it. All of her false bravado from earlier abandoned her, and Athena realized in a nauseous rush that she couldn't handle horror movies yet.

Her stomach did a second backflip and she spewed again, more chunks of her dinner splatting down to the ground. Her friends, who had been so quick to chase her outside, now took big steps back,

Simon's hands in the air as if he was surrendering. Behind them, the ticket seller in her booth started banging on the glass.

"Get her away from the theater! I'm not cleaning that shit up!"

Shelley, being the good friend that she was, tried tiptoeing forward, around the flecks of vomit, but when Athena twitched, Shelley jumped back again. Shelley was wearing her nice jacket. Her best Converse. Maybe she'd just give Athena a second to work all of this out of her system.

Athena was crying. She felt the hot streaks of tears coating her cheeks as warm globs of stomach acid clung to her chin. The theater's doors banged open behind them, and Athena heard a familiar voice start reassuring the ticket seller.

"I'll get her out of here. Yes, her and her friends. I've got it."

Dad? Athena thought. But there was no way. He was passed out, sawing logs on the couch at home.

Athena raised her head and, despite her tear-blurred vision, managed to recognize Mr. Collier. He looked different in street clothes. Less formal. Less authoritative. But she would recognize that firm hand on her shoulder anywhere, and Mr. Collier squatted down in the puddle of Athena's bile, holding her steady to help her regain her composure.

Shelley, still standing clear outside the splash zone, shot daggers at the Assistant Principal's back.

"You okay, Athena? I saw you rush out of the theater and thought... well. I thought something was wrong. What are you doing here?"

"What are you doing here?" Shelley interjected.

"Huh?"

"Did I stutter? What are you doing here? Are you following her?"

"Huh? No. I was watching a movie."

"Convenient." Shelley hissed.

"Jeeze, kid. Adults have lives too." Mr. Collier scowled, debating Shelley without ever taking his eyes away from Athena.

"Yeah, and you just happened to be in the same theater we went to, at the same showing of the same movie?"

"I guess. Sure."

Shelley raised her eyebrows and looked back and forth from Athena to Mr. Collier, and back to Athena. Meredith and Simon took another set of steps backwards, wanting no part of whatever was about to break out here.

"You buying this, Athena? Girl. There's a killer on the loose and our assistant principal is just popping out of the shadows-"

"- I was already in the theater, seated and looking forward to a calm night before you four snuck into the back row."

Athena just shook her head and wiped her lips dry using the sleeve of her shirt. There was too much going on. She couldn't think through this right now. She sort of understood what Shelley was suggesting, but she was too disoriented to really care at the moment.

"Stop it, Shelley. It's fine. He's fine."

"Bullshit."

"Hey!"

"I've seen these movies. I know how this goes. The supposedly innocent side character who just keeps popping up all over the place. They're always the killer in the end. This is one of those plotlines, isn't it, Mr. Collier? Or is that even your real name?"

"Kid. Seriously. Stop. Athena, are you okay?"

Athena nodded, but she did so slowly. Uncertainly. Mr. Collier released his grip on her shoulder and rose, stepping back from Athena and turning to face Shelley directly.

"You need me to help drive you home?"

"Not on your life, Mr. Collier."

"Kid. Chill. I'm trying to help."

"Uh-huh. Like you helped Marco?"

Mr. Collier froze, a look of frustration and disgust plastered on his face.

"I'm fine, Mr. Collier," Athena insisted, and she rose as well, stepping between the assistant principal and her friend before either of them did something regrettable. Meredith and Simon bustled to help and grabbed Shelley's shoulders, both whispering for Shelley to shut the fuck up.

"We're going home, Mr. Collier. I'll see you in school… whenever I'm allowed back," Athena tried to break up the group. Mr. Collier stared down Shelley, anger clear in his eyes, but he kept it trapped there. Maintained his composure otherwise.

"Going home sounds like a great idea, Ms. Hammond."

"But the movie!" Shelley griped.

"Seriously?" Simon asked, gesturing at the chunky mess Athena had made.

Shelley groaned, frowned, then regained her composure also, like Mr. Collier, stepping forward to grab Athena's hand. She pulled Athena away from the adult with a little more force than was necessary.

"Fine. We're going home. Maybe stop by CVS to get Athena some mouthwash because damn, girl. We've got her from here, thank you so much, Principal Collier." Shelley said the last part as sarcastically as possible, but Mr. Collier didn't take the bait. He just stood outside the theater, watching the kids usher their friend away into the night.

"I swear. It's him. He's gonna turn out to be the killer."

"Shelley, I swear to God if you don't shut up."

"But for real. It's standard slasher rules. Like I said. All we've gotta do now is figure out who he's coming for next. Quick, somebody say 'I'll be right back,' then walk down that alley!"

"Shelley!"

"Do you think Marco drank? Or had sex? Had to be one or the other."

"Stop it. We're freshmen."

"Well you're all freshmen. Marco and I are Juniors. Remember? And didn't Marco get held back a year in Elementary School? The guy was practically an adult."

Was.

The word hung in the air, heavy enough to have its own gravitational pull. The past tense sucked the life out of the group and Meredith frowned. Athena bit her lip to keep from crying. Athena looked at her friends, terrified. How many of the rest of them would be gone before this thing settled?

"Shit, Shelley, he just died last night. How are you already so callous about this?" Simon called out.

"Because! The killer is still out there. Don't you guys get it? This is no time to be retrospective and mourning. We've got to look ahead. Need to figure out how to defend ourselves! So here we go. We're gonna head back to my house for a slasher movie marathon. My Heart Is A Chainsaw, Friday the 13th, Nightmare on Elm Street. All the classics. And we're gonna figure out Mr. Collier's pattern before he can-"

"Stop! Shelley. This is too much."

Shelley shot daggers at Athena.

"Athena, how did you survive at Camp Tall Pines? How did you stop all those killers at once? There's got to be some trick we can use, right?"

Athena dropped her head down, ashamed to think, even for a second, that Shelley was right. Lamenting the loss of their friend and pretending like all this wasn't happening was foolish. It had been dumb of her to come out here tonight, pretending like the world would just let her reset her life. If Mr. Collier had been out to get her, like Shelley said, then she was giving him the perfect opening.

And keeping secrets about what happened at Camp Tall Pines? Not letting the others know what they were up against? It was selfish.

"I hid," she whispered to the gravel underfoot.

The others all stopped walking and turned towards her. This was the first time she'd told anybody about the massacre besides the detectives and, as ashamed as she was to not have a better answer, she felt the words start bubbling out in a rush, unable to keep it all in. She'd been hiding so much for so long, even the tiniest crack in the dam of her resolve led to an eruption. A flood of revelation and confidence.

"It was horrible. Everybody was dying and I didn't know what to do. They lined all of the other campers up in a circle. Cut them down with some ritual knife. Chainsaws. Machetes. You name it. And I hid. In my bed. Under the cabins. Under potatoes."

"Under potatoes?" Simon asked, but Athena ignored him.

"I heard everybody else screaming, but I just ran and I hid. I can't help us here, Shelley. I'll tell you everything I know about this cult, but I feel so useless. All I can do is run. Hide. Get out of the way."

"If all you did was hide, then who killed all of those cult members?"

Athena didn't answer at first.

Shelley stopped walking and grabbed Athena, pulling her in for a tight hug, despite the flecks of vomit on her hoodie. Simon and Meredith whispered to each other, both of them looking stunned like deer in headlights. They didn't want to be here. Didn't know how to react to Athena in the moment. Athena couldn't blame them.

"There's no way. Your dad? ...Unless...What the hell happened at that camp, Athena?" Shelley whispered into Athena's neck, their faces buried in one another's hair, seeking and giving comfort back and forth.

"I can't..."

"Athena, whatever is happening here. It's affecting the people around you. It's affecting your friends. It got Marco already. We need to know what we're up against. If Mr. Collier back there had been after you, we need to know how to help you."

"I..."

Athena took a deep breath. She thought about all the times her dad had told her, back at camp, as the police flooded in, to stick to their story. No matter what they had to stick to their story. Telling the truth would confuse them. Confused people tend to react poorly. We don't like being confused. And that had made sense, surrounded by a bunch of strangers with badges. But these were her friends. These were the people she needed to be able to trust.

"There was a monster."

Simon and Meredith's eyes went wide like goldfish.

"I fucking knew it," Simon whispered, and Meredith elbowed him in the ribs. They had all stopped walking now, on the outskirts of town, halfway home under a flickering street light. Athena looked up and down the street, making sure it was empty. Then she met Shelley's eyes.

"There was a monster. It was inside my dad and it made him do things, awful things, to the camp counselors. The cultists. That monster helped us survive. It killed every last one of them. It gave us a way out. But now I'm worried about what it cost my dad. He's been so strange since we came back. So reserved and secretive. I don't know if the monster took part of his soul, or if he's just messed up from the part he played in everything, or..."

Athena's hands were shaking and she stuffed them in the pockets of her hoodie, hoping the others couldn't see how much of a wreck she was.

"I tried to get him to go see a therapist, but he's not into it. Instead he's just thrown himself into this project building out the basement. He stays down there for hours, but even when he comes back up, he's like a shell of his former self. Therapy didn't work. He never snapped back and I miss the old him. And if all of this is starting back up again, I can't lose him."

"You mean you can't survive the cultists without the monster?" Shelley asked.

"No. I mean I can't survive it without him. The monster killed, but he saved. I need him back."

"What kind of a monster?" Simon asked, and again Meredith elbowed him.

"Not the point," Meredith mouthed. Simon just shrugged in response.

"No, no. Simon is right. We need to know what kind of monster," Shelley pushed the conversation along.

"It doesn't matter. It's dead."

"Did you watch it die?"

"Sort of. No. I guess not. But my dad exorcized it somehow."

"Exorcized it? Like a demon?"

"Yeah. I guess."

"The news made it sound like it was just some slasher. Not a demon possession."

"I guess it was a bit of both?"

"A good slasher never dies. We should have known there would be a sequel."

"Simon, shut UP."

"So what do we do? If you survived last time by having your dad get possessed, then what's the move here?"

"Find the demon?" Simon suggested and flinched, anticipating another elbow jab from Meredith. But none came.

Wind shook the branches overhead, sending them clacking into each other like a wave of nature's own applause. A shower of acorns and dead leaves tumbled down around them, and a bat chased a moth through the glow of the moon.

Shelley looked from Athena to Simon to Meredith, a smile playing across her face.

"Find the demon."

Chapter Fourteen

Boone

When Boone woke the next morning, he felt inspired. Angry still. Frustrated. But also validated. Motivated. He knew that the cultists were back and that all of his investigations had been justified, and now he just had to bunker down, dig through the clues from Jolene's house, and pinpoint the bastards down.

He walked upstairs first, tiptoeing up the creaky wooden steps to check on Athena. Finding her tranquil. Fast asleep in bed. Her window was open, which gave Boone a brief moment of pause, but he snuck through the room and, after closing it, checking her closet, and checking under her bed, he convinced himself things were fine.

She must have just wanted to sleep with some fresh air blowing in.

Boone went down to the kitchen and made some coffee. He checked out the front window to confirm that, yep, the cops were still swarming the place, their barricade still holding back the press. But the press were thinner now, and the police seemed less high strung, he thought. Boone popped the cap off of a dry erase and wrote a note to Athena on their fridge.

"Basement day. Come get me if you need something. Love you."

He poured himself some coffee, left it black, and made his way downstairs.

For all the time he'd spent down here, it felt like he'd barely made any progress. Construction tools littered the benches. Boxes of tiles and huge squares of soundproofing foam and dry-wall lay near the back, all in varying states of preparation, but hardly anything had been set in place yet. In the middle of it all, a metal chair sat unfolded, the only piece of "furniture" that had made its way down here so far. Boone sidestepped the chair and tilted one of the soundproofing sheets forward so he could fish out the bag which had been stashed behind it. Not the most secure hiding spot, but of course, Boone hadn't been expecting the entire Bayside police force to show up on his doorstep the day before. He'd have to find a better hiding spot before he wrapped up today.

He pulled the zipper. Saw Jolene's yellow mask staring back up at him from the darkness of the bag, guarding the secured wooden box that he'd confiscated from her house. He stared down the mask, glaring at darkness behind the eye holes, half expecting Jolene's enraged glare to materialize there for ritual's sake. He knew this wasn't the same mask from camp. How could it be? And yet he still envisioned the thing coated in blood, dripping red as Jolene stalked towards him, wooden bleachers and pine cabins ablaze all around her, Athena dead on the ground behind her.

He picked up the mask carefully and set it aside. Reached down instead for the padlocked wooden box. He retrieved a hammer from his toolbox and smacked the lock once, twice, three times, stripping the screws free from the wood and causing the whole mechanism to fall to the concrete floor in an unhinged heap. The metal clank reverberated through the basement like a gunshot and Boone paused, his attention directed upstairs, listening for any indication that he'd woken his daughter up.

But there was nothing.

No creaking bed springs and no pitter-patter of teenaged feet headed for the pantry.

Perfect.

Still in the clear, Boone swung the lid open to find a book. Boone pulled the book out and looked all around the inside of the box, hoping something else might be hiding in some nook or cranny. But there was nothing. Just a book, sealed away.

He let out a frustrated hiss of air.

There had been books all over Jolene's room. Who the hell cared about another book? It wasn't even a journal where Jolene might have spilled her secrets. He had those already. It was just some stupid library book with "Rooker Public Library" stamped clearly on the front cover.

'ALL AMERICAN LEGENDS' the title proclaimed, with a picture of Native Americans crowded around a campfire, the smoke rising overhead and making a shape like a shadowy figure watching over them all.

Boone walked over to the folding chair and sat down, opening the book on his lap and flipping through a few pages. The thing read like a textbook, covering a seemingly random assortment of supernatural beings that had been reported throughout American history. It started with a tour of Native American tribes and their mythos, then built to the colonists, touching on some aspects of the witch trials, then culminating in pictures of Bigfoot, the Jersey Devil, Mothman, and some other cryptids. ALL American Legends was over-selling it, but they certainly covered a wide assortment of the bastards. 623 pages deep, Boone noted. A chunker of a book. Boone flipped through the pages quickly, barely glancing at more than the titles and the pictures.

This was stupid.

Nothing was highlighted. Jolene hadn't left any little hand-written notes in the book. It was just a bunch of bullshit conspiracy theorists throwing their daydreams around. Except Boone knew that wasn't true now, didn't he? As crackpot as he'd always believed UFO-lovers and satanic cultists and whatever else to be, he'd seen with his own eyes that there was something else out there. And if Jolene had been so committed to this book that she'd locked it away in a secret room in her closet, then something in here must have been connected to Camp Tall Pines. He would just have to... and he hated this. Truly loathed it with every inch of his being... He would have to read.

Boone cursed and stomped his foot like a child throwing a tantrum.

"What a waste of time," he grumbled, but he flipped the book back to page 1 and, in the dim light of the basement that he was supposedly working on, Boone began working his way instead through the text.

Chapter Fifteen

Athena

She Googled it. She actually freaking Googled it.

"How to find a demon"

Meredith, you idiot.

"What, do you think a demon is out here checking our browser history?" Meredith threw her hands up in the air, befuddled.

"No, but the cops could be." Shelley snapped.

"Shit. Forgot about them."

"You forgot about the cops? What did you think all those blinking lights outside the window were?"

The four friends had reconvened in Athena's bedroom, Shelley, Meredith, and Simon all slipping under the hole in Athena's back fence and climbing the tree in her back yard to join her, unnoticed.

"I mean. What are those cops even really doing? We all got in here without being spotted. If they aren't even monitoring the outside, you think they're monitoring the inside?"

"Maybe they've got one of those white vans parked up the street with a bunch of tech guys piled inside. They tapped the phones and are watching the Wifi and-"

"-watching the Wifi?"

"I don't know how any of this works, but maybe we shouldn't be meeting here?"

"Yeah. This is gonna be the safest spot around. The boys in blue aren't gonna stop a demon, but they could at least slow one down. And they would keep the Cultists busy if they came for us. Probably. Either way, they buy us a little more time to escape than we'd have anywhere else. Right, Athena?" Shelley suggested.

Athena just shrugged.

Her mental funk from last night still hadn't lifted, even after sleeping in that morning. She was glad that she had told her friends everything, but now the heavy noose of guilt hung around her head. When her dad found out that she'd blabbed, she would be in so much trouble. And her revelation about how she'd survived? Actually voicing out loud that all she'd done was hide? It ate at her. What had she done to deserve to live that Elena hadn't? Her daddy had come to save her. Her parent had bailed her out. What sort of validation was that?

"Hey! Athena! You with us?"

"Yeah, yeah." Athena put on the best smile she could muster and tried to stay focused on the present. This could be her chance at redemption if she could stand up to the cultists. Help save her friends. Winning now wouldn't fully justify her walking away from Camp Tall Pines while nobody else did, but maybe it could be a start.

"So I see this as a four step plan. Right?" Meredith stepped up. Shelley was the sparkplug of the group. The one who got everybody invested in an idea. Meredith was the planner, though. The one with the intelligence to actually slow down and to think something through. The pair stood at the front of Athena's bedroom like drill sergeant prepping the infantry before an invasion. Athena and Simon sat on Athena's bed, quietly letting the others piece things together. Nodding whenever Meredith or Shelley turned to ask their opinion about something.

"Step One: We find the demon. Step Two: We find the Cultists. Step Three: We find a way to lure the demon to the Cultists. Step Four: We stand back and let them hash it out."

"Sounds great," Athena said, unconvincingly. Shelley and Meredith shot her a look.

"What? What's that tone for?" Shelley asked. "Come on. You're the expert here. If we've got something wrong, speak up before more people die! Sheesh. No. Wait. I'm sorry. That was harsh. But seriously. Why don't you sound convinced?"

"Because you haven't seen what the demon can do."

"We've heard the stories. We've read... yeah. We've read the newspaper articles. Assume we've got a sense of the destruction a demon can cause. Why not turn that against the Cultists?"

"Because you can't just 'turn' a Demon on a person–"

"--group of people–"

"I know that! But this Demon is freaking smart. The way my dad talks about her–"

"--her?--"

"--Yes, her. I guess. Shevra. But my Dad said it was like she was toying with him the whole time. Like she could have taken control of him at any point, brought the whole Cult and the whole Camp to its knees at any point, but instead she messed with him because it was... I dunno... fun? We can't just walk into something like that unprepared."

"Where IS your Dad?"

"We won't be unprepared!" Shelley turned on her heel and grabbed a bag from the dresser behind her. She pulled out Blu-Ray after Blu-Ray. The Exorcist. The Taking Of Deborah Logan. The Curse of the Reaper. She tossed them out on Athena's bed one by one.

"I dunno if this is such a good idea. After the way Athena lost it last night?" Simon said, frowning at the movies.

"No no no. This will be better. Possession movies aren't slashers. They're totally different subgenres. Very few bodies hitting very few floors. Its mostly mental. Which is perfect. It's what we need. To get in the headspace of people standing up to a Demon."

"I thought we were standing up to the Cultists. Where's Rosemary's Baby?"

"Ew. Athena is like, 16."

"What? No. Just for fighting a Cult in general. Jesus."

"One step at a time. We'll figure out what's going on with the Cult later. Demon Theory first and foremost." Shelley asserted, and without any further discussion, she grabbed the Exorcist from its sleeve and popped it into Athena's Playstation.

"Now pay attention, kiddos. Take notes. You've got a lot to learn and precious little time to learn it. We need clues about where demons come from, how they choose their victims, and what powers they've got once they're inside them."

"I want popcorn."

"Then go make popcorn," Shelley said, but she didn't pause the movie, instead settled back against Athena's bed and let the movie spin up.

On the bed, Simon reached over and squeezed Athena's hand. He gave her a look that asked 'are you really okay?' without actually asking it, and Athena nodded. If they were going to go demon hunting, then she'd better be able to make it through a damn movie. No panic attacks and vomiting. Not this time. She needed to be strong enough to protect her friends. Like Shelley had said, she needed to take things one step at a time. For her, Step One was watching a scary movie. Preparing herself for what was to come. Step Two, she would face her demons.

Chapter Sixteen

Boone

Upstairs and in the basement, the Hammonds spent the day reaching the same conclusion. Their research was fruitless. Three possession movies and hours of reading books from the library led Athena and Boone to the same dead end- whatever information they had been seeking, they were going about it the wrong way.

For Athena and her friends, the movies revealed nothing resembling a common theme. Apparently demons just possessed whoever they wanted, whenever they wanted. Young girls, old ladies, priests, you name it. Shelley kept trying to draw threads between them, but her logic felt like a stretch. Grasping at straws and seeing patterns that weren't really there. A conspiracy theorist trying to cheat off other people's homework.

In the basement, Boone read through chapter after chapter, periodically standing up and banging on things with a hammer so that Athena wouldn't grow suspicious. She was being awfully quiet upstairs, but maybe that just meant she was sleeping the day away. After his fifth time hammering, Boone stood in the corner of the room, arms crossed over his chest, staring back at the book where he'd laid it on his chair. It shone in the light, glossy cover shimmering like a video game item you were meant to notice, pick up. A video game item that would progress the narrative, show the character some clue that would let them into the next phase of the story.

It was mocking him.

"Fuck you, book." Boone growled.

In his head, Dr. Carver chastised him. He was externalizing his feelings again. It wasn't the book's fault he had reached this dead end. The book was just an object, like the Cultists at the camp had just been murderous psychopaths. The Cultists didn't make him crazy. The book didn't make him a failure. He just needed to breathe, take his time, and focus.

But no.

Screw all that.

Boone crossed the room and kicked the shit out of the chair, sending it flying across the room in an outburst. The book flew too, its pages flapping through the open air like it was a baby bird trying to leave the nest too soon, crashing down to the concrete limp and lifeless. In its wake, a library card drifted through the air.

Bayside Public Library. Stamped twice, with Jolene's name and...Caroline's?

Hold on.

Boone picked up the card and investigated it. Checked the dates when the book had been checked out and back in. Jolene had taken it a year ago. Caroline had taken it a month prior. Then nobody for four months before that until Kyle. Weren't those all names of the killers from camp? Not just Jolene, but Caroline and Kyle too?

The wheels in Boone's head started turning, slowly at first, but gaining steam.

The library. If Jolene had borrowed this from the library, then the library would know what other books she'd borrowed. And, more importantly, it would know who else had borrowed the same books. There would be a literal paper trail for him to follow. Dots for him to use to connect one Cultist to another and another. There could be a whole network of weird, murderous teenagers just waiting to be ousted.

Boone scooped the book off the floor and hurried upstairs. He stuffed the card back into the book, tucked them both under his arm, and snatched his keys off the table.

"Athena! Baby! I'm gonna head out to the grocery store for a bit. Need anything?"

He heard a yelp from upstairs, like he'd surprised Athena.

"Um…nope. I'm good. All good," she responded, and Boone heard her trying to suppress a giggle, but didn't think much of it. Teenage girls were weird. "Thanks for asking though. See you in a bit."

"You betcha," he called back. And with that, Boone jumped in his truck, cranked the keys through his ignition, and pulled his truck slowly, carefully, out of the garage and past the reporters that littered his front yard. He kept his windows rolled up and only made eye contact with the police officers, nodding to them as casually as possible.

"Just going out for groceries," he tried to communicate with his nod.

"Nothing to see here. No reason to get suspicious. Just a dad on his way to restock a pantry."

Once through, he drove haphazardly around town for the next five minutes. Turning his left turn signal on a few times before he turned right, pulling into parking spaces only to immediately pull back out, his eyes focused on his rearview mirror the entire time to make sure he wasn't being followed. To make sure nobody was doing the same maneuvers he was. There was one beige car that might have been a cop, but he lost it long before he pulled into the library's parking lot, rolling to a stop in the back of the lot, out of view from the main road. Nobody would know where he was going or what he was looking for. Perfect.

Boone stepped out of the car carefully, winding his keys so they jutted out between his fingers, past his knuckles. Weapons at the ready, just in case. He stepped into the library on the highest level of alert.

Chapter Seventeen

Detective Ramsey

Detective Ramsey sat in his motel room, pictures and interview notes spread on the small, water-stained desk in front of him. He'd spent the day running around the town like a chicken with his head cut off. Interview after interview with people who knew the Hammonds, or at least who claimed to know the Hammonds, had led him to the same conclusion over and over, though it was a conclusion he didn't like. A conclusion that didn't fit with the bigger picture.

Boone's fire captain described him as a hard worker, sure, but just the kind of guy you liked having around the station. Personable, positive, even on the worst days, even after the worst calls, he'd be the one able to lift everyone's spirits. Not a jokester or anything like that, but just a really solid guy. Not, as Detective Ramsey had surmised, the type of person to murder a camp full of children.

Athena's Principal had been a dunce. More interested in saying something that might turn into a news headline than in saying anything straight-forward or honest. Ramsey had tried to explain to the man that he was a detective, not a reporter, but the Principal's grandiose showmanship had never wavered and it all escalated to the point where Ramsey wondered if the "show" he was putting on wasn't really a show. Maybe he was genuinely so naive and self-centered.

"Of course, Athena is wonderful! Like all the students here at Bayside, she put her best foot forward every day, and..."

"Why, here at Bayside we teach all of our students about the value of every human life. Children come in all shapes and sizes, with different talents, and Athena is just one more ray of sunshine that helps form our rainbow of academia."

Ramsey tried to stay objective with his interviews, basing his opinions exclusively in facts. It was important in his line of work to be able to separate his own feelings about a person from the pictures that the proven details wove. But in the principal's case, the details had shown the man to be a total, pompous, gas-bag.

But he'd turned Ramsey on to Assistant Principal Collier. So that was something at least.

The AP had been more reserved with the Detective. Cautious, like he didn't trust the man which, ironically, made Detective Ramsey trust the AP even more. He didn't turn on a faucet of faux school spirit at the first question. He kept his answers close to the chest. Chose his words carefully.

Ramsey liked the man.

They had sat in the AP's office for over an hour, going back and forth, Ramsey whittling his answers from the AP slowly, one at a time.

"What was Athena like?"

"In middle school? Sweet as can be. She had a couple spats with other girls in her class, but it was always the other girl who started it, always one of Athena's friends who finished it. Athena herself never raised a finger against another kid. Wasn't in her. Couldn't tell you now-a-days, though. I was gonna try to figure her out, help her find her feet again, but she was only here for a single day."

"Who were her friends?"

Collier had frowned at that.

"Elena Rodriguez was her closest one. Best Friends Forever sort of a thing. But she...well..."

Ramsey just nodded.

"Then there's Shelley Fitzgerald. Who is a firecracker." Collier's eyes faded as for a moment, Ramsey lost the man to a memory. Some event which caused Collier's brows to furrow. "They talked in middle school, but it looks like they've gotten a lot closer since. I guess she's the closest thing to a friend Athena came back to. There's Meredith Sherman and Simon Pawlowski, too. Together, the three of them might be worth talking to. They'll know Athena from a more kid-to-kid perspective. I know Athena's told me a lot over the years, but I'm an adult. No telling how much she's held back from me..."

Detective Ramsey raised an eyebrow, but said nothing. He made a show of writing down the three kids' names, but kept his attention trained on Collier. Gauging his actions. Watching the color return to the man's knuckles as his grip on his arm rests relaxed.

Curious.

"You have pictures and addresses I could get for those kids?"

"We aren't allowed to give that out to the public."

"Good thing I'm not the public."

"Yep. Guess you're right about that."

Collier clacked at his computer for a few minutes while Detective Ramsey sat quietly, watching the man until a printer churned out reports on the three students.

"Appreciate it,"

"Yep."

"So, final question. In your opinion, could Athena have murdered anybody?"

"No chance in hell."

"Her father?"

"Never met the guy, but Athena loved him. No hints of abuse or domestic violence or anything. Always seemed like a perfect little family."

"Perfect. Great."

And that was the problem, wasn't it? Detective Ramsey thought as he pored over his papers and notes. The perfect little family that he saw on paper didn't match up with the psycho killer family that he needed for his storyline to make sense. There should have been signs. Murderers, especially the big serial-killer ones, usually had criminal records. Minor incidents, at least, that wouldn't have forewarned anybody about what the killer was capable of, but which looked like breadcrumbs in retrospect. The people around them would have reported things being 'off' from time to time. Even the killers that masked their true selves the best would slip from time to time. Show their true face to the people around them. Again, not so obviously that people would put the pieces together until afterwards. But this WAS afterwards, wasn't it? This was the time when the puzzle pieces were supposed to start making sense. Hell, even the dead wife didn't seem to lead anywhere. He looked down at the coroner's report from her autopsy. Car accident. Totally on her own. No foul play suggested. The driver of the semi truck had been drinking on the job and had no relation to the Hammonds whatsoever.

So what the absolute fuck was going on here?

Ramsey slumped back in his seat and tapped a pen against his teeth.

Tomorrow he would interrogate the children. Find out if Athena had some skeleton buried in her closet that the adults hadn't been privy to.

But part of him knew that wasn't the case. Part of him knew the real killer was somewhere else. Hiding. And what was worse was that, for some reason he couldn't explain, he also knew that the killer was close. He was the idiot in the movie with his gun trained on the door while the killer walked up from the shadows behind him.

He desperately needed to figure out which way to turn before it was too late.

Chapter Eighteen

Boone

The library is almost perfectly empty except for a family of four in the children's sections. Boone stands at the front desk, hardly ten steps from the front door, in a standoff with the late-40s, scruffy-bearded librarian who was manning the station.

"I told you, that's not information we can give out to the public."

"And I told you that I'm not the public. I'm Jolene's uncle. I found this book while we were cleaning out her things and wanted to return it."

"Then return it."

"I will, but I was also hoping to see what other books she had been checking out. To see if...maybe...we could piece together what happened to her."

The librarian just dead-eyed him, not buying the story for a single fraction of a second.

"Dude. Are you a cop?"

"No. Fireman."

"Because if you're a cop, you have to tell me you're a cop."

"No. What? That's not true. But I'm not a... ugh... Listen, man. Jolene is dead."

"Yep. You mentioned that."

"And the rest of our family, they're all hung up about it. Nobody ever really talked to her or paid attention to her. And we're all just looking for a little bit of closure. Some way to connect with the niece, the daughter, the sister, we missed out on really knowing. And you're telling me there's no way you can help us piece that together?"

"Nope."

Boone groaned, mentally. A voice in his head told him to go into Camp mode. Just muscle through the nuisance and take what he needed. The computer was right there. The librarian was already logged in. It wouldn't be too hard to figure out how to search a patron's name, find their checkout history, right?

But Boone glanced at the family in the children's section, their toddler pulling book after book from the shelf, and he shook the thoughts away. No Hulking out. Not with them here.

"Tell you what, man. You give me the book back," the librarian held out his hand. "And I'll scan it into the system, see what I can find, and see if there's anything about your 'niece' (he used his fingers for air quotes) that I can tell you without the rest of your cop buddies jumping down my throat."

"Not a cop," Boone reiterated, but he passed the book over reluctantly.

"Of course not." The librarian flipped the book open, found the library's barcode stickered inside, and shot it with the scanner from his desk. He squinted his eyes and rolled his mouse around, clicking here, humming there, until he pulled his face away from the screen, satisfied with whatever he'd found.

"Your girl was a bookworm."

Boone cringed, inwardly, at the insinuation that Jolene was 'his girl' but kept his emotions off his face.

"Buuuncha books here. Some weird stuff that I can't tell you about," the librarian winked at Boone and Boone wanted to pummel the cocky bastard more than ever. "But here's what I can say. We've got a book club meeting tomorrow. 7:30. In the basement. Seems like, if I was trying to learn more about my dead 'niece' I would want to talk to the people that new her best, right? And based on the number of times she came here for that book club? Pretty decent bet the kids there knew her.

Suddenly all of the resentment Boone felt towards the librarian melted away.

"7:30 tomorrow night?"

"Have you ever known teenagers to do stuff at 7:30 in the morning?"

Boone ignored the man's sass. 7:30 would be right after his next appointment with Doctor Carver. That was perfect. He could go see the doc, make sure his head was on right, maybe prevent himself from doing anything brash and stupid. She'd know how to keep him on the level. Then he'd come to the library to take care of business. The pieces of the plan fit together like jigsaw pieces, clicking into place effortlessly, the big picture starting to come into focus for him. The end result taking shape. A finale. A way to cut this cult out at the source. A chance to get some peace of mind for himself and for Athena.

"How many? Kids in the book club I mean."

"Hard to say. Used to be a lot more, but their numbers seem like they thinned recently. Mind you, I just let them in. They're regulars around here, so Jimmy just lets them lock up after themselves usually."

This was it. The motherload. Had Boone actually found ground zero for this stupid cult? Was this where everything started? He looked around the library again, really assessing his surroundings with a critical eye. Rainbows were painted over the children's section. Was there anything sinister about the rainbows? Anything satanic about where they started or ended? A poster for the Twilight Saga, more than a decade old, hung over the Young Adult section. Was there a connection to glittery vampires?

No. He was being stupid. Even if this was ground zero, he couldn't start conspiracy theorist spiraling. Stay focused. The book club. He would come back tomorrow night to investigate the book club. He wouldn't act on them. Not yet. Probably. But reconnaissance. Learn first, forewarned would be forearmed. Then he could make a plan to eradicate evil from its source, once he knew the whole picture of what he was up against.

He was so lost in his daydream about what was to come that he almost forgot to thank the librarian, who saw the distracted look in Boone's eye.

"You stay safe out there. Sorry for your 'loss,'" he said, air quotes again.

Boone nodded. Grumbled a thank you. Exited the building, head still in the clouds.

The librarian pulled out a sticky note, immediately regretting telling the strange man about the book club. He hadn't seemed threatening until he heard about the club. But that look in his eye as he walked out the door?

JIMMY- STAY AROUND FOR BOOK CLUB TOMORROW NIGHT. WEIRDO ASKING AROUND ABOUT IT. LOCK UP FOR THE KIDS AND GET A SQUAD CAR TO ROLL PAST?

He taped the note to the bottom of the monitor for Jimmy to find tomorrow, then leaned back in his seat, flipping the just returned back open and diving into the stories of chupacabras and witches. What kind of weird stuff was that book club into, anyhow?

Chapter Nineteen

Boone

Boone pulled past the dwindling numbers of reporters and cops, up his driveway, and into the safety of his home just after dark. It was good to see the siege outside thinning. Reporters were getting bored, realizing the Hammonds were just a boring family trying to lead boring lives. And as the reporters left, the police's numbers were able to shrink as well. Tonight, Boone only saw one police car and two vans from local cable channels sitting at the end of his driveway.

"Good. Get lost." he whispered to them as he passed.

He closed the garage door, maneuvered through the tight space between his hood and a wall of gardening tools, and reentered the house through the kitchen, tossing his keys onto the island and heading directly upstairs. He wanted to tell Athena what he'd discovered. Dad was making headway here. He was going to keep her safe again, and if she could just hold on one more day, he'd have all this wrapped up with a neat little bow on top.

He opened her door without knocking which was, even he knew, a cardinal sin in the teenage years.

Three kids nearly leapt out of their skins, eyes wide at the sight of him. A fourth kid, a boy, was asleep in Athena's bed, and Boone nearly jumped out of his own skin at the sight of all the intruders.

"What the-"

"Dad! Hi!" Athena called, quickly, jumping from atop the bed.

In the corner of the room, Athena's TV showed scenes of some monstrous looking lady swallowing a person whole. A found footage camera jumped around as people out of shot screamed, and the two other kids who were awake, Michelle and Shelley, Boone recognized them now, seemed like they were about to have a pair of panic attacks between the movie and Boone's sudden arrival.

It was a movie night.

Boone's heart rate dropped a couple hundred beats per minute, levelling back out to normal. He released his grip on the doorknob, realized he had squeezed the shit out of the hunk of metal, like he was preparing to rip the door off its hinges to swing it at the unexpected guests.

For the briefest moment, Boone had seen everybody in the room wearing those damned masks. He'd envisioned Athena, dead on her bed, with the cultists here to finish the job.

And he'd been ready to annihilate every last one of them on the spot. Had he dented the fucking doorknob?

Boone closed his eyes. Forced himself to take three deep breaths.

"Hey, baby. What's...uh...You're not supposed to have anybody over. How did your friends get past the police?" He stepped back. Looked down the hall, towards where blue lights could be seen flashing through the front-facing windows, an ever-present strobe to accompany their daily lives.

"There's a gap under your fence. Where the creek comes through," Michelle confessed.

Boone groaned. He'd never even thought about that. He was building a panic room in the basement before he'd ever bothered to walk the perimeter of the property, check for the obvious points of entry.

"Hi Michelle. Thank you. I'll take care of that."

The kids' faces dropped and Shelley shot Michelle a 'how could you' sort of a look. No more sneaking around and coming to see their friend. They'd have to use the front door like normal people. Poor kids.

"Shelley"

"Mr. Hammond."

"Athena, who is that?" Boone pointed to the boy on the bed. Athena looked over at him, then looked back at her dad, cheeks flushed with red at the realization of how the scene must have looked. A boy had snuck into their house, climbed into bed with her.

"No, Dad. That's not the way it-"

Michelle caught on and started laughing, unable to help herself.

"Oh, God. No. Mr. Hammond, that's just Simon. He's not. Oh, shit. Is he asleep?"

"Nothing bad is happening, Mr. Hammond!" Shelley jumped in.

Athena just stood in the middle of the room silently, dumbstruck. It looked like she wanted to crawl under her bed to die from embarrassment.

Boone could have been a jerk. Could have tried to teach her some lesson on the spot, or tried to scare the teenage boy, or any other number of stupid alpha dad moves. But no. He remembered Simon from grade school. The kid had rocked a bowl cut to Athena's 6th birthday party. His parents both worked at the University two towns over. Boone didn't need to mess with the kids' good time.

"What are we watching?" he turned the conversation, and Athena breathed an exaggerated sigh of relief.

"Horror movies!" Michelle called out.

"Well yeah. I see that. Athena, are you good with these?"

There was a moment of reckoning behind Athena's eyes. She looked to Simon again, then back to the TV, then back to her dad.

"Yeah. It's...I dunno. Helping? Like a practice run for the real thing or something."

Boone nodded.

"Well if you're good, then I'm good. Just... he doesn't sleep there tonight." he pointed a big, calloused finger towards Simon, still asleep on the bed.

The three girls looked at each other and goofy, embarrassed grins crawled across Michelle and Shelley's faces.

"Sure, Mr. H. We'll make him sleep in the closet."

"Or on the roof."

"Drape him over a branch of the tree like a leopard or something."

"I'll bet he still doesn't wake up, even then."

"Hah! Yep."

Michelle and Shelley joked back and forth as Athena regained her sense of normalcy, recovering from the shock of her dad bursting in.

"Good night, everyone."

"Night, Mr. H."

Boone winked at Athena who mouthed a silent 'thank you' in his direction. Athena needed this. More than she needed police officers in front of their house, or a panic room in the basement. She needed normalcy. A murder at the school had robbed her of that. Boone wasn't about to take another thing away from her. He could tell her about the library in the morning, after all of her friends had some breakfast and left, and–"

Shit. He never had actually made a grocery run. Did he even have food downstairs for the teenagers to eat?

He closed the door slowly, gently, glancing at the other three kids one more time as he did. Michelle was standing up, facing Simon, a devious look in her eyes that suggested she was about to play a prank on their slumbering companion. Athena was twisted about, watching her, the color in her cheeks reverting back to normal. But Shelley was watching Boone. Staring right back at him until the door latched shut. Looking at him like she knew something. Like she suspected something. There was a slight sparkle of familiarity behind those eyes, and after the door closed, Boone's instincts would keep him up for the rest of the night.

Chapter Twenty

Athena

In the morning, Athena's dad made everybody an eclectic breakfast of toast, cereal, coffee, and a few poptarts. He'd obviously just scavenged what he could from the pantry, and Simon was the only kid who drank coffee, but they all feigned manners like the gesture was overwhelmingly generous and well thought out.

There was a tension in the air, making the whole meal awkward as shit.

Simon was quiet while he ate, but that was typical for him. Especially after the girls had told him about the encounter from last night, the one he'd slept through, Simon wasn't about to speak up, or say anything to draw extra attention to himself.

Shelley sat at the end of the island, and also barely spoke all through breakfast, which, unlike with Simon, was wildly unlike her.

Meredith helped cut the tension by talking about how all the movies last night had been stupid. The Exorcist playing up Catholicism as the only religion that could stand up to a demon. "What did they corner the supernatural market or something? Where's all the Jewish Exorcists?" and carrying on and on. Athena's dad spoke to the kids in short, choppy, one-word answers, despite "making" breakfast for them all and seemingly trying to put on a show as host. His smiles never reached his eyes. There was something guarded there. Calculating.

"So what's the plan for today?" Athena asked, trying to break the ice some. "Dad? Are we still on house arrest?"

Boone shrugged.

"Dunno. That detective hasn't come back by. Most of the police cars are gone from the front. Maybe?"

"You think they'd tell you something like that. Give you the all clear or make sure you were in here like you were supposed to be or something," Meredith offered around her mouthful of Poptart and strawberry filling.

"We aren't under arrest, so I think there's limits to how much they can bother us. Right, dad?"

Boone shrugged. Disconnected. Distant. His mind clearly somewhere else.

Athena frowned.

"Well it doesn't matter. We've got a movie marathon to finish, don't we, everybody?" Shelley asked, putting a little extra emphasis on the phrase movie marathon as if enunciating might hide what she was really saying: research so we can find a demon.

But the rest of the kids were over it.

"The movie marathon was dumb, Shelley. We watched four movies last night and we're no closer to figuring out what the rules are for-"

Shelley shot Meredith a look that could have killed and Meredith caught herself. Bit her tongue, glancing at Boone's turned back.

"No closer to figuring out what the rules are for the genre. Mrs. Hopefield assigned us this brutal project where we have to study a whole trope from a genre, then write an essay about it, THEN write our own story that fits the rules. It's brutal, Mr. H. Language Arts shouldn't be this hard."

Meredith winked at Shelley who just rolled her eyes.

"Good save," Simon mouthed right before Boone turned around.

But all the secrecy made Athena feel awkward. She didn't want to keep secrets from her dad. In fact, maybe he could help them. If the demon had been in his head before, maybe he knew things about it that the movies wouldn't know. What had Mrs. Hopefield called it in the one class Athena had attended with her? Primary Sources instead of Secondary Sources? Go to the people that had actually been there, done that?

"What are you up to today, dad? Wanna watch some with us?"

Shelley kicked the shit out of Athena's shin.

'No adults!" she mouthed.

But Boone wasn't paying attention. He just stared into his coffee as he sipped it.

"Can't. Busy today. Gotta... work on the basement."

"Oh. Well. Okay then. If you're busy."

Athena rose from her stool and began awkwardly backing towards the stairs. Simon and Shelley, both eager for the group to regain some privacy, followed along with her, and only Meredith stayed in her seat, looking pleadingly from her friends to the food still on the table. She sighed.

"Fine, I'm coming. Thanks for the grub, Mr. H!"

"What? Huh. Yeah. You're welcome. Have fun, kids. Stay inside. Stay out of trouble."

"Always do," Shelley called.

Athena turned and led her friends' stampede up the stairs, seeing her dad shake his head as they left, clearly not believing Shelley's words.

Chapter Twenty One

Boone

Boone cleaned everything up downstairs and polished off a second cup of coffee, listening to the teenagers upstairs. It took them an hour to turn a new movie on, instead giggling and shouting and messing around, loudly, behind closed doors. The way teenagers were supposed to. Boone kept reminding himself that all of this was normal. Poorly kept "secrets" from parents. Hiding in rooms with boys. He should have been thankful for all these little worries. But instead, Boone found himself distracted by the big picture. The damned cultists.

He would take care of them tonight, one way or another. He'd been up all night plotting exactly what that might look like. He would go to the library after the meeting started. He would sneak as close to the proceedings as he dared, phone on audio recorder. And the second those bastards said anything concrete, he was going to save the recording, call Detective Ramsey, and let the authorities come swooping in. Boone wasn't stupid. Without Shevra rippling through his body, he knew not to go confronting a pack of cultists all on his own. Didn't know if he had the stomach for it. Knew he didn't have the biceps for it. Maybe if there was just one or two of them, then he could…

No.

No!

By the books this time.

He had toyed with the idea of just telling the police outright. Letting them do the whole raid, start to finish. But Detective Ramsey wouldn't trust him on this. And if he turned out to be wrong, then he would blow his own cover. Let the Detective know that he had this whole side project under way, and all the security around Boone would be beefed up to an 11. No, he had to make sure that the Cultists were actually there first. Had to make sure that when he made that call, the cage would come down around all of them without a single crack for the snakes to slip through.

He glanced at his watch, saw that he still had hours to kill before his appointment with Dr Carver. Surely she would agree with this plan, right? He wasn't going into harms way, not directly. He was getting closure for himself so that he could move on. That's what she had encouraged in the last session, wasn't it? See this thing through just a little bit farther, then get out once things were secured.

He wondered if she would tattle to the police. Wasn't there some sort of a mandatory reporter clause in all of the paperwork he'd signed in their first session? He couldn't remember.

He put his mug in the sink and washed it out, the door to the basement catching the corner of his eye.

Maybe he would actually go to do some work down there. Get a wall up or something, like he'd been meaning to. But then, if everything really did end tonight, in the library, then what would the panic room be for? Maybe he could actually use the basement as extra space? Build a home theater or something.

He decided to spend his few hours before the appointment down there mulling over the possibilities. He went into the basement and closed the door behind him, blocking out the sounds of his daughter and her friends overhead.

Chapter Twenty Two

Therapy

The tape recorder crackles along at full speed, half of the session already over with. We can hear Boone talking slowly, really weighing each of his words as Dr. Carver 'Mmm's and 'Aah's in response.

"So I think that's the best move, right Doc? And as an added bonus, I'll be there when the cuffs get slammed on the monsters. I'll get to see them taken away. No hearsay. No relying on other people to tell me what happened. I think that'll help solidify my peace of mind."

"It's an interesting idea."

"Interesting?"

"Boone, I can't tell you what to do. I certainly can't condone behavior like this."

"Like what? I'm just going to a public building and listening in on a conversation. I think the 'It's a free country' line is bullshit, but...isn't it?"

"You're walking in there alone."

"Right."

"At night."

"Right."

"And you don't have a plan to bring a weapon with you?"

"No. I don't plan to get into a fight with whoever is there. I just want to go in, get my evidence, and get out."

"But what if they catch you?"

"Then I'll run. Know my exits and all that. Keep the truck parked facing the street and keys in hand. Keys would be a good weapon though, right? Wind them between my knuckles? Fire station used to advise that in a self defense class we took, but I've never actually tried it."

"Boone. You're not thinking clearly."

There's a long pause on the tape, little sparks of feedback popping and cracking, keeping uneven time, letting the listener know the tape hadn't just stopped.

"You're right. This is dumb. I should just tell the police."

"What?"

"Yeah. I'm trying to go all Rambo here or something. This is dumb. I got so caught up in all of this that I'm not thinking straight. I'm putting myself, and I'm putting Athena in danger, and I've been trying to justify it by telling myself that I'm trying to protect her, but in reality, I'm just too pig-headed to ask for help."

"No. We've been talking about this. You're doing the right thing. You need this closure to..."

"But that's just it, right? This won't be closure. This would just be perpetuating a cycle of violence. I don't want to bring a weapon to that library because I know that I'd use it. I know that I'd try to go full camp mode again and I'd try to solve my problems by just bashing brains in. But that didn't work last time. That wouldn't work this time. Clearly there's something bigger at play here than just dropping a few more satanists or demon worshippers or whatever. These kids are organized. How did they get so organized? Maybe I'm just chopping off heads of a hydra and there would never be an end to it. But Detective Ramsey? He could bring the whole institution down. Whatever it is that's going on here, he could bring in the kids for questioning, get some answers, really find the poisoned roots of this whole thing and pull shit up by them."

"Shit."

"Um… language, doc?"

"Don't do this, Boone."

"I'm gonna call Ramsey. Maybe he'll let me tag along in the squad car. See the kids get taken in. Shit, he probably won't let me out of his sight whether he's letting me tag along or putting me in the car for his own satisfaction. But either way I'll see, you know? And once he slaps the cuffs on whoever's in that basement, Athena will be safe."

"I really thought we were gonna get there without having to resort to this, Boone. I really did."

"Huh?"

The tape recorder screams. It's an inhuman sound, like feedback blaring from a bad mic check. Except there's something animalistic in the sound. Something gnarled and coarse and ancient about the shriek. Something that shakes the listener's bones, makes them question everything they know about humanity, nature, and the universe. Heaven and Hell grinding against each other like nails on a chalkboard.

Detective Ramsey reaches out and turns the device off.

Chapter Twenty Three

Athena

They're halfway through their second movie of the day, Jennifer's Body, but Athena can't take it anymore. She jumps up and grabs the remote and turns the movie off. Meredith cries 'hey!' waking Simon up again. Shelley glances up from the phone she's been staring at, sending text after text to…somebody. Doesn't matter. Athena's done watching movies.

"We aren't getting anywhere with this."

"Says you! Simon's getting at least three months of his beauty sleep back," Meredith joked, and she poked her friend in his groggy little face.

Simon slapped at her.

"So what do you propose we do instead?" Shelley asked, lowering her phone, but still keeping it in her hand. Not pocketing it yet. The screen flashed a few times as she received texts and Shelley's eyes wavered back and forth from Athena to the device.

"Hypothesize. We've seen five movies-"

"-four and a half-" Meredith corrected.

"Fine. Four and a half movies about possessions. What have we learned?"

"Demons are fucking wild. And you fought one?" Meredith asked, leaning forward, leaving Simon alone.

"What? No. Not really. Jolene fought one."

"The dead counselor that tried to kill you."

"Right."

"And she tried to kill it with a chainsaw?"

"Yes, but stop. Focus."

"That must have been wild."

"WOULD YOU LISTEN? I think I've got something here."

"Oh?" Shelley leaned forward now too, phone flipped upside down on the carpet beside her.

"What've you got, girl?"

"What do all of the possessed victims have in common?"

"Nothing. Literally nothing. We watched three girls and two guys get possessed. We watched children and teenagers and old people go down. There's no thread."

"Stop being superficial and think about the person."

The other three friends sat still for a second.

"They're all…"

"Broken."

"Huh?"

"They all got possessed in some moment of critical weakness. Jennifer as she's dying. Reagan in her childhood. The common thread is that the demon finds somebody vulnerable, and that's their way in."

"So when the demon possessed your dad?"

"He'd been stabbed by a cultist. He was bleeding out beside the lake and I guess the demon found him there. He doesn't talk about it much, but I'm pretty sure that's how it went."

"Wait. This makes sense."

"So who is weak around here?"

"Well AP Collier is a little bitch,"

"Shelley, shut up. Seriously. Who do we know that's been struggling? Somebody who, I guess physically or mentally, has needed help. Who might have reached out to somebody, or something, and accidentally given them an opening to..."

"...Maybe somebody that went to therapy, but it didn't take...?" Simon asked, his voice a soft whisper.

It clicked with all the kids at the same time.

Athena's dad. The one who had been self-isolating for months. The man who seemed so hollow. So distant. Athena had chalked it up to him struggling to process the events from Summer Camp, but what if his shifted demeanor wasn't really *his* shifted demeanor. He hadn't been himself since they got back home.

That's the way Athena had described it to her friends, wasn't it?

Hadn't.

Been.

Himself.

"Oh, fuck!" Meredith put it eloquently.

The teenagers all spilled from Athena's room, chasing each other down to the basement that Boone had supposedly been working on for months. The basement where he spent most of his time alone, with nothing but his own thoughts. The basement that was completely empty now, with nothing but a single metal chair and a book in the middle of the space and some drywall boards leaned up in the corner. The basement with absolutely no sign of Boone Hammond now.

Chapter Twenty Four

Boone

When Boone came to, the first thing he noticed was the smell of copper. It flooded his nostrils, made him feel queasy, clouding out all of his other senses for his first few moments of consciousness.

Then came the sticky warmth, all over him. Running up his arms, down his cheeks. He realized that he was kneeling, and because he was kneeling, the whole bottom half of his jeans were coated in liquid, heavy, mess. He had only been in the library's basement one time, while doing volunteer work with the fire station, but he recognized the space immediately as he forced his eyes open.

"Welcome back, bitch."

It was Dr. Carver's voice. And yet it wasn't. It was something far more eternal than a simple doctor. It had gained a depth, a vibrance, that Boone had only heard once before.

"Did you miss me?"

"No. No. No. No."

Boone forced his eyes open further, the sticky substance on his face resisting him, trying to keep the lids glued together. Don't look at this, the adhesive said to him. You don't want to know.

But the drying blood eventually gave way to Boone's insistence, and Boone took in the gallery of gore which surrounded him.

They were in a room with no windows, the only light coming from a flickering bulb overhead. The bulb swung wildly, as if something had just slapped it, sending it windmilling in insane pseudo-circles, spotlighting different aspects of the carnage with each heave and each ho.

An arm lay on a table in the corner, the skin peeled back from around the elbow like a half-eaten banana, blood seeping out across the surface it lay upon.

Somebody's ribcage, still intact, but sans any skin or internal organs, had landed on a coat rack against a different wall, hung like a lampshade over the top of the stand.

Two flayed bodies were situated in the center of the room, bones cracked so their torsos could be folded around to make a heart shape, their feet the bottom point, their heads and necks touching to make the crack in the top. "Missed You," written in gore between the pair.

Boone threw up, adding his own bodily fluids to the cocktail mixture all around him.

"Oh, come on, man. I thought you'd appreciate this!"

"Why are you back?"

"That's a funny way to say 'Missed you too"

"Shut up. Get out of my head. Why did you come back?"

"I knew you needed me."

"Bullshit. Why did you come back?"

There's a long pause. Dr. Carver, Shevra, doesn't seem to want to say. But she's in Boone's head again. Boone's head, and he knows from camp that means he gets a little bit of a window into the demon's mind too. These possessions worked both ways.

He pried. Saw the world. Freedom. Running through the woods, terrifying young couples on camping trips. Then he saw weakness. Saw power draining, dwindling, suddenly, out of nowhere, like a plug had been ripped out of the bottom of a bathtub. It got harder to breathe. Harder to move. It felt like it had when Shevra first crawled from the lake. When she found Boone. Boone. Boone. She had needed to find Boone again, and...

"You were dying."

"Shut up."

"You were dying and you came back into me like a goddamn parasite!?"

"Something went wrong. The ritual was complete. I should have been free, but something went wrong. I thought you might know what. So yeah, I came back. I watched you and Athena from behind your eyes. And you know what I found?"

"I couldn't possibly care less. Get out of my head."

"I found you two in danger. Again. And you don't even realize it. You need me, Boone."

"I need you gone." If Boone had been in control of his own tear ducts, he would have been bawling at this point. How was he in this situation again?

"As your therapist, I strongly advise you to grow a pair of ovaries and step the fuck up. Athena's in danger. And I know exactly how many shits you give about her. So here we are, Boone. You need to protect Athena. I need to figure out why I'm not at full strength again. Lets team up. For old time's sake."

"No. Get fucked."

"Too bad. So sad. You don't get a say. Shoone rides again! Or. No, that sounds stupid. Bevra? There we are. Bevra rides again! Now quick, grab that blinky brick off the floor."

"Blinky brick? You mean the phone?"

"Yeah, sure, whatever. It's been flashing at us for the last, like, half an hour."

"Fuck!" Boone followed the flashing light, bone fragments and body tissue crackling and squelching underfoot as he walked, the bulb still swaying overhead, keeping his vision patterned and inconsistent. Like the world's slowest strobe light, the situation around him kept taking shape one blink at a time.

Here was a foot, ripped in half, two toes on one segment, three toes on the other. Here was a clump of hair. One of the cultists had been scalped, it would have seemed. And then, in the corner, right next to the phone, was the mound of masks. The teenagers must have brought their disguises with them. Planned to wear them during their meeting like some fucking larpers on their way to roleplay DND in the park.

The masks were multicolored, just like the ones at camp had been. The blues, greens, and yellows brought back memories of stalking through the woods. Preying on one after another. Some deep, dark, sadistic part of him felt sad that he'd missed the hunt this time around. Shevra had already dispatched all of them while Boone was unconscious. Hadn't she?

"How many this time?"

"Twelve."

He thought about the number. Thought back to camp.

"There was one missing, wasn't there?"

"Bingo bango wango tango. Thirteen masks, twelve dismantled meatbags. Somebody didn't show up for the costume party."

He picked up the phone.

"I have an awful suspicion I know who it was…" Boone bemoaned. And looking at the dead cult member's phone only served to reinforce his fears.

SE: ITS THE DAD. YOU WERE RIGHT, BROCK

BK: SHIT. I KNEW IT. WHERE?

SE: GOTTA BE THE LIBRARY. I DON'T KNOW
HOW HE WOULD KNOW ABOUT THAT, BUT
IT'S GOTTA BE WHERE HE WENT.

BK: YOU HAVE THE DAUGHTER?

SE: ATHENA'S WITH ME. YEAH.

BK: GOOD. I'LL TELL ELIJAH

AND I'LL BE RIGHT OVER

SE: BRING BACKUP

BK: ALREADY PLANNING ON IT. NC/SC
CHAPTER SENDING SOME PEOPLE OVER.

SE: WHY ISN'T DANIEL RESPONDING?

BK: PRIVATE MESSAGES. NOW.

"They're coming?" Shevra giggled.

"They're coming," Boone said.

Chapter Twenty Five

Athena

Athena and her friends made their way through the woods as quickly as possible. Which was to say, very slowly. Cutting through the woods to the library was the most direct route from Athena's home, but with the sun setting and visibility dropping, and logs to climb over, and creeks to leap across, they probably would have been better off just sprinting the extra mile along paved roads and flat sidewalks.

Athena made the trek with her phone out, watching as the GPS from the "Find My Phone" app brought her closer and closer to her father. It had been Boone's idea to install the app on each other's phones. Part of his overprotective drive. But it was working out in Athena's favor now, wasn't it?

Why was her dad at the library though?

Athena stared at the dot, pinging consistently in the same spot. Up ahead, Meredith slipped in a patch of mud. Behind them, Simon moaned and complained.

"Girls, slow DOWN."

"Keep up, Simon. We're almost there."

"Quit your whining and come on. We need to warn everybody at the library!"

Athena felt so stupid, thinking he'd been working in the basement this whole time. Why hadn't she gone down there a single time to check on his progress? She should have known something was up with him, but she'd been so self absorbed. So excited to get back to school. She hadn't bothered to give her dad a passing thought. Of course he was fine. He was her big, strong dad. Nothing ever went wrong with him. She got in trouble, he bailed her out. That's just the way the world worked.

But now, the prospect of the tables being turned gave her pause.

If their theory was right, and Shevra had returned to her father again, then what did that mean for everything else going on around Bayside? Had her dad been the one who killed Marco? Probably. Only the demon would have butchered her friend that way. Staked him up like that on the football practice sled.

But even if that was true, and Athena knew she was making some big leaps in logic, it still didn't explain *why*?

Back at camp, the Demon's rage had seemed targeted. Focused on the cultists. So did that mean...? Is that why there had been a wolf mask at the crime scene? Had that mask been Marco's?

There was no way. She'd known Marco far too long. He couldn't have hidden something like that from her, right? Except she didn't really know Marco that much. He'd been a fringe friend, hadn't he?

"We're here!" Shelley called, the faded red and brown bricks of Bayside Library coming to view through the tree-line. As they approached, they saw the parking lot. Saw Boone's truck parked there among a dozen or so other cars.

"Holy crap. He's actually here," Simon gasped, catching up behind the girls. They all crouched down, dropping to their knees, eyes fixed on the front door.

"So what do we do? Trap him inside and call the cops?" Meredith asked, looking at Athena as if she was suddenly the leader of the group.

"No. No. There's no trapping him inside. He'll go straight through those glass front doors, no matter what we do."

"We call the cops!" Simon offered.

"Oh, HELL no," Athena snapped. That'll just be more casualties for the crossfire."

"So what do we do?" Shelley glanced at her phone. "It's nearly 8:00."

"And?" Simon asked.

"I dunno. The library's supposed to close sometime soon, right? Maybe that means we wait here and see if anybody comes out to lock up?" Shelley suggested.

"Maybe Boone's just in there tooling around. Athena, you should go in and just look around real quick. If your dad sees you, then you could just go, 'Hey dad! Found any books on exorcisms?" Meredith tried.

"Wouldn't that just be a Bible?" Simon asked.

"Shut up, Simon! You get it, though. If he's in demon mode, he won't attack you."

"But he'll know you left home and you'll get in trouble. He'll know we're onto him. Or the demon will know we're onto them, right? We've still got the element of surprise right now. We can't squander that by going wandering into the library. We should stay out here, watch, and wait." Simon and Meredith went back and forth.

"Shut up, Simon!" Meredith hissed.

Athena tried to tune out her friends' bickering. They both had points. Athena was so worried about what was happening to her dad, but if they were wrong about any of this, then wandering in there could be a death sentence. At camp, her Dad had, somehow, managed to use the demon to protect her. But maybe that had been a one time thing. If the demon was back, and it was in that library, then there was no way of knowing how they would react to the sight of her, the last sacrifice from camp.

"Shelley, you should go," Athena finally said. "He knows you pretty well, so if my dad's possessed, then he wouldn't attack straight away. He recognizes you enough to trust you. He'd protect you, I'm sure. But also, if you left our house and went to the library, he wouldn't question it. You just got bored of watching movies or something, and you could walk in there without drawing any serious suspicion, just in case things were going sideways." Athena suggested.

"OR you came to get more movies. Just tell him that we finished the one we were watching, and you needed to check out some more." Meredith offered.

"Yes! Okay. Got it. Good cover, we'll roll with that." Athena.

"You can get movies at the library?" Simon asked.

"Simon, I swear to God if you don't focus the fuck up," Meredith threatened.

Shelley seemed to think about the idea for a moment. She rose and dusted some leaves from her knees, checked her phone again, and glanced towards the front doors.

"I'll go poke my head in. See what I see. But if you hear me say to run, then you run. Got it?"

The other three all nodded their heads.

Shelley crept forwards, emerging from the woods and trying to look casual as she approached the library's front doors. She pressed her back flat against the bricks, then craned her neck around to look through the glass.

All of the kids jumped when the motion sensor triggered, the outermost doors sliding open with a whoosh.

Shelley glanced back at the others, glanced in to the library, then slipped around the corner, disappearing into the darkness without a word.

Chapter Twenty Six

Athena

"She went inside!?"

"She wasn't supposed to go inside!"

"I know that. Shit. What do we do now? Follow her?"

"I guess. Maybe. I don't hear her screaming or anything. And if it looked dangerous, she would have come running. Would have told us to run, right?"

"I would think so."

Athena, Simon, and Meredith crept from the woods, following the same path Shelley had taken towards the doors. Meredith led the way with Athena close on her heels, Simon snagged on a bramble, but hustling to catch back up.

The library past the doors was dark. No lights were on save for one emergency light that could be seen far, far away towards the back of the building.

"Shelley!" Meredith whisper yelled at the barely observable outlines of bookshelves.

"Why the hell would she go in there?" Simon asked, actually whispering.

"Maybe she saw somebody?" Athena offered. But it was a weak idea. Meredith and Simon both looked at her, and she shrugged.

"Well. Lets go get her, I guess." Meredith grumbled.

Athena took a step back.

"Nope. We need to go get help. Libraries aren't supposed to be dark like that."

"It's closing time."

"But we didn't see anybody close up! Something's wrong. We need the police."

"Hello, Mr. Policeman? We can't find my dad, the lights are off in the library, and our friend is trespassing. Send all units!" Meredith mocked.

"Don't gaslight me," Simon argued, standing up for himself for the first time in weeks. "Marco is dead. The cops know shit is funky around here, and they'll take this seriously. Come on. Shelley went in there on her own, she can find her way out on her own."

"Help!" Shelley's voice came from inside the library. Weak. Distant. Like it was at the end of a tunnel, and Simon's argument died on his lips. He groaned as, plucking up all the courage she could muster, Athena pushed past Meredith and bullied her way into the library.

There was no sign of Shelley. She was gone. Vanished without a trace. That should have been Athena's first warning sign. But contrary to every survival instinct that had propelled her through the Camp Tall Pines Massacre, Athena pressed forward. Even as she knew she should dive beneath a book case. Hide under the bed in the medical ward. Save herself and wait for the danger to pass, instead this time she forced herself, step by step, to enter the darkness.

Shelley was worth it.

The only friend Athena had left from 'the good old days.'

Meredith and Simon came up on Athena's shoulders. The angels of the good new days, watching over her, peering into the shadows along with her.

To their rights they could see the light from the stairs leading down to the basement. The light glowed softly, outlining the mostly-closed door.

"Does that light look red to you?"

"Shut up, Simon. Stop being paranoid. It does not...oh shit, it looks red, doesn't it?"

"Shelleyyyyy" Athena whispered, louder this time.

They needed to get out. Nothing about this situation was good. They had put their foot directly into the bear trap and were teasing the spring with their little toe.

There was a crash followed by the sound of little pricks of glass rattling down atop some bookshelves at the back of the library. The emergency light vanished.

"Dad?" Athena tried whispering instead.

Beneath her feet, she felt the ground shift, ever so slightly.

"What the FUCK was that?" Meredith screamed, her voice piercing through the previous silence-fuelled tension. And, as if Meredith's scream was the signal everybody had been waiting for, the world broke open around them.

Huge writhing tentacles tore through the floorboards, bits of human bones, flesh, and organs flying up along with it. In a flash three, four, five tentacles, splashing orange viscous fluid, flooded the library, swinging around blindly like a child trying to hit a pinata.

Meredith dove to the floor. Athena threw herself sideways, into the History section. Simon wasn't so lucky. Catching a tentacle in the hips, Simon was thrown up into the air, caught by a second tentacle, and slung into the children's section. He screamed as he landed, a pained noise, but a noise Athena was thankful to hear. Noise meant he was conscious. Noise meant he might live.

From the back of the library there was a flash. Then another flash. Then another. Shelley stood, her back against the wall, phone out, camera popping away, capturing image after image of the tentacles.

The ground shifted again, chunks of flooring and sections of shelving plummeting into the opening, tumbling down into the basement as Boone Hammond ascended, raised up by tentacles which had torn through his shirt, spouting from dislocated elbows, shoulder blades, one even emerging from his ankle.

For Athena, this was old hat. Jarring, but not world changing. For Meredith, her cry of panic suggested she might never regain her sanity again. And still, Shelley stood by the back of the library taking pictures.

What the hell is she doing?

Athena glanced at Meredith. "Get down and stay down!" Athena ordered, then began sprinting across the library, feet dancing around the holes in the floor, eyes trying to adjust to the minimal light, but Shelley's flash disorienting her every time it went off.

"Shelley, run!"

There was an emergency exit right beside Shelley. Why wasn't she diving through it? Saving herself? Why was Athena having to run across the library to save her?

Another flash, and Athena saw the smile on her friend's face.

Nothing about this was catching Shelley off guard. No, the smile on her face said this was what she had wanted. What she had been hoping for?

"...Shelley...?" Athena gasped, and she slid to a stop a few feet shy of her...friend seemed the wrong word at this point.

"Little Wolf Pup, look at you." the demon said from behind Athena. Its voice had hints of Boone's voice built in, but it was more than that. Layers upon layers of cosmic warbling distorted the sound. Made it feel like the voice was worming its way into Athena's skull instead of just being vibrations in her ear drums.

"Did you plan all of this? Was it you who brought me back?"

Shelley just smiled. She stepped up closer to Athena, who was too dumbstruck to react. Shelley grabbed her former friend and spun her around, held a kitchen knife up to Athena's throat. Where had she seen this before?

"They're coming for you now. They're coming for you and Elijah will be so proud of me. Little old me, from Bayside, Virginia. Who would have thought? Who would have known?"

"Shelley. Whatever's going on here, I promise. It's not too late to-"

Shelley's knife bit into Athena's throat

"Don't you speak, you cowardly bitch. I've had to listen to you for months now. Whining. Complaining about how hard it was to be the sole survivor from that camp. You should have just died there. Shut yourself up so we wouldn't have to listen to you feeling sorry for yourself."

Athena opened her mouth to say something, but thought better of it. Instead, she turned her eyes towards her father, with all of his tentacles waggling around like Doc freaking Oc in those Spiderman comics. His eyes were cold. Full of hate. He wanted to kill Shelley. Wanted to rip her apart. It was like she could hear his thoughts.

Wait.

She could hear his thoughts.

Move, child. Give us a clear shot.

That wasn't her dad. That was the demon. Was Athena talking to the demon in her mind.

Athena thought about it. Felt some outside force nudging her along. Encouraging her to move. But no. She wouldn't out her friend like that. A good friend wouldn't have ever put a knife to her throat like this, but still. Maybe this was somehow a misunderstanding. If Athena could just get everybody outside, into the fresh air, maybe they could talk this out.

"Elena should have come back. She was the smart one. She was the nice one. Not you. Not some nobody like you."

Shelley sounded like she was talking more to herself now than to Athena. Applying a little bit more pressure with the knife, Shelley pulled Athena backwards towards the Emergency Exit.

"What did you do to deserve to get back here? You hid. That's what you said. You hid and you ran."

"Move, child. Give us an opening."

But Athena couldn't. Wouldn't.

"Shelley, please."

They were nearly at the Emergency Exit now. Shelley could probably dive through the door before the tentacles got to her. Depending on how fast the tentacles were.

"Move."

"No."

"No time like the present to give the Devil what he's due, huh?"

Shelley spun Athena around, raised the kitchen knife into the air, and tried to bring it down into Athena's forehead.

But Meredith had been on the move, crouched low, sneaking into the Encyclopedia's section. The book she threw came spinning through the air, hurled like a bullet, and its hardback spine struck Shelley in the side of the head, knocking her attack off-center just enough to miss Athena's face. Instead, the dull knife found the soft flesh of Athena's shoulder and, blunt as it was, the force of Shelley's swing was enough for it to punch through the skin.

"Athena, no!" Boone and the demon shrieked from the middle of the library.

Shelley dropped down, recoiling from where Meredith's book had struck her, then she spun, slipped out the back doors right as Boone's tentacles slammed into the space she had been occupying. One of the tentacles caught Athena's foot, breaking it at the ankle, and Athena shrieked in redoubled pain.

Shelley disappeared into the night. Her phone lay beside the encyclopedia that Meredith threw, but one glance at the screen told everybody that the damage had been done.

The last text message Shelley sent was still on the screen. A picture of Boone, emerging from the basement. Tentacles slipping past torn skin.

The reply, from 'BK,' said they were on their way, locked and loaded. Elijah Hanson would be so proud of Shelley.

Chapter Twenty Seven

Athena

Sounds of the onset of nighttime drifted through the open door at the back of the library. Grasshoppers sang, birds chirped goodnight to each other, and there was a constant whoosh whoosh whoosh sound of cars rushing back and forth along the nearby road, with people headed in from work, or out for a night on the town.

In the library, nobody made a sound. They all just sat there, staring at each other, trying to figure out what to do next.

Simon, whimpering, finally cut through the tension.

"My chest. It hurts."

"Yeah, bud. They threw you through a bookcase. I'll betcha you snapped a few ribs."

Boone and the Demon looked over at Simon and contrasting displays of pity and amusement rippled across the hybrid's features. Athena scowled.

"It hurts to breathe."

"Broken ribs. I'll bet ten bucks."

"Make it twenty?"

Meredith nodded. Yep.

"Why are you back?" Athena demanded, just like her father had.

She was addressing the demon for the first time. Even at camp, with the Demon rushing this way and that way, piloting her father around, Athena had never had a chance to speak to the thing. Make any sort of contact with it. Doing so now felt wrong. Speaking to her father, taking a tone with her father. But it wasn't her father. But it was.

"You. Something about you, child. We sacrificed you at that camp, completed the ritual, and I got to be free in this world. But that freedom waned. My shackles weren't all the way removed, it wouldn't seem. And now I've got the old ball and chain back." Boone and the Demon hugged themselves, and Athena saw a look of disgust cross over her father's face.

"So. If you don't mind, lets just kill you again and I'll be on my merry way."

"Absolutely the fuck not." The response came from Boone's body, but the tones were slightly different. Less coiled mass of dying animal sounds. More the sound Athena had grown up listening to and trusting.

"One, we're not killing my kid. Two, she was alive at the end of Tall Pines. She's alive now. She's a constant variable. Whatever changed, dragged you back into me, it wasn't her."

On the ground, Meredith and Simon both stared at Boone, horrified to the brink of insanity, but holding it together for the moment. They looked over at Athena when the Demon mentioned her dying, but Athena shook her head like it wasn't some big thing. But her dismissiveness just made her friends' incredulity deepen.

"Dad. Demon," Athena spoke up.

"We prefer to go by Bevra now,"

"No we don't," Boone responded, and Athena's head spun, watching her dad argue with, it looked like, himself. His mouth flew and contorted to make two competing sets of sounds, sometimes simultaneously as his and the Demon's arguments overlapped one another.

"I'll call you Dad and Demon, fuck you very much. Gods, were you two like this last time?"

"No."

"Yes."

"What is happening?" Simon asked from the ground.

"Nothing good, dude." Meredith offered.

A chunk of the library's floor broke away, falling into the crater that led to the basement, bringing a shelf of books- the Romance section- along with it, and Meredith slid Simon a little bit farther away from the center of the library, closer to the back door.

"We need to get the fuck out of here!" Meredith yelped, pointing towards where Shelley had vanished with her chin. I'd really rather not see what's making that stench in the basement.

Boone and the Demon smiled, glancing back at the hole.

"Yes, yes." And the gang all hurried outside, Boone leading the way and glancing around to make sure that Shelley was actually gone before ushering the others through. They held the door for the kids, and for some strange reason, Athena got the impression that it wasn't her dad holding the door, it was the Demon. Shevra. Faking chivalry and then bowing to the children as they came through. This was all way too freaking weird.

Bevra closed the door behind everybody, withdrawing their tentacles now that they were outside where people might see them and freak out. They squeezed the door's handle and snapped it off, effectively locking the place down, then started leading the way to the front door.

Meredith and Athena grabbed Simon by the shoulders, helped him walk to the front, struggling to keep pace with Boone who made it to the glass double doors and flipped the library's sign around from 'Open' to 'Closed.'

"Really?" Meredith asked.

Bevra shrugged and smiled.

Everybody in the truck. If those assholes are closing in on us, we've got a few stops to make. Dying child, would you like to waste everyone's time going to the hospital? Or can we go straight to the crematorium?

"Wait. What?" Simon gasped. His face, which had been flush red since the injury, suddenly drained all of its color."

"She's screwing with you, kid. You're fine. First stop is the hospital. Meredith, can you call Simon's mom? Tell her where we're going?" Boone asked.

"Of course, Mr. H."

"No details about what happened. He fell down the stairs at our house. Just leave it at that," Boone instructed.

"Classic," the other half of Boone's mouth said.

"Shevra, would you shut up?" Boone yelled at himself.

"Dad, would you please stop talking?"

Athena helped her friends climb into the bed of the truck, then slipped into the passenger seat. Boone slid into the driver's seat and fired up the engine, waiting to hear a 'thump thump' from the bed, Meredith signaling that she and Simon were situated and ready to ride.

"You see, girl? This is why we don't invite boys over. They sleep in your bed one time and the whole world can go to hell."

"Shevra, seriously. Shut up," it was Athena who called out the Demon this time, and it felt oddly satisfying to snap at the thing.

They turned left out of the library's parking lot, Boone intentionally driving slowly, taking the turns easy so as not to jostle the teenagers in the back too much. The hospital wasn't too far away, and the roads between here and there were recently paved, smooth by Bayside standards. They coasted along in silence for a few miles.

"So. What do we do, Dad?"

Boone breathed deep, eyes never leaving the road.

"We need to know what's going on here. The Demon and I bashed our way through two waves of these fuckers, but they keep coming. We need a new strategy."

He drummed his fingers along the steering wheel and glanced at a Home Depot they were driving past. There was a shooting range across the street. WalMart a couple stores down.

"Lucky us, we know they're coming this time. Maybe we don't know much about them, or what's coming, but at least we know our battleground. It's our turn to pick the conditions of combat, since they have to come to us."

"So we're going to fight them again?"

"Of course, girl!" the demon chanted through her father's lips. She began singing, "Blood, blood, buckets of blood…" with a manic glee, but Athena's father's eyes never changed. Never grew cloudy, the way they seemed to do when the Demon took control of him. Instead, he stayed sharp, focused, in control of everything except his vocal chords as they pulled up to the hospital. Meredith and Simon climbed down from the truck's bed, Meredith closing the tailgate and giving the vehicle a quick double slap, letting Boone know they were good.

Athena watched her friends leaning on each other, Simon moving slowly, carefully, making sure he didn't jostle his injuries too much, Meredith with her shoulders under his armpits, helping him along. Athena wished she had gotten out with them. She wished she could be there for her friends, and wished her friends would be there for her right back. But that wasn't the hand she'd been dealt. Shelley was the worst. A wolf in sheep's clothing of the most literal degree. She had gotten close to Athena solely so she could hurt her.

Athena was starting to understand her lot in life now. Friendships. Childhood. Carefree days spent skipping rocks into a lake at Summer Camp, or carefree nights going to see a movie with her friends at the local theater were all just fantasy for her now. For whatever reason, the gods had decided her life was headed down a different path. There would be no friends, save her father Boone. There would be no 'carefree' anything. At least, not as long as these Cultists stayed around. Not as long as this Demon kept her father tethered to them.

Athena watched her would-have-been-friends pass through the sliding glass doors of the hospital. Saw the medical staff rushing forward with a wheelchair. And she knew that was the last time she would see either of them. Two paths diverged in a yellow wood, and

Athena was pulled kicking, screaming, clawing, fighting, and finally, dejected, down the one nobody else traveled.

Chapter Twenty Eight
Boone

He'd grabbed the one with the squeaky wheel. Gods damn it.

Boone wandered up and down the aisles of Home Depot, scanning up and down each impossibly high rack of shelves, searching for inspiration. Shevra joined him, watching through his eyes, yelping excitedly whenever something particularly sharp or demented came into view. Even objects that Boone would have never considered to be 'weapons' piqued Shevra's interest, and the limits of her creativity made Boone feel sick to his stomach.

"What's that?"

"A post hole digger"

"Grab two."

"Fine."

"What's that?"

"Lawnmower. It cuts grass."

"Is that all it can cut?"

"Um...no."

"Three of those."

"Shevra, three lawnmowers won't fit in the cart."

"We'll come back for them, then. I like them."

It was like negotiating with a toddler. Every time Boone tried to say 'no,' Shevra threw a tantrum. Took control of Boone's features and threw whatever it was in the cart despite him.

Watching them argue must have gotten under Athena's skin. She excused herself and went to the opposite side of the store, presumably looking for a nail gun, most likely just trying to get away.

"Remember, Shevra. We're looking for non-lethal damage. We need these guys alive so we can question them."

"Yeah, yeah, yeah. I'll keep one alive."

"Two. Just in case."

"Sure sure. Two. Whatever," Shevra said, but the way she spun a welding torch around in Boone's hands made him suspicious.

Athena reappeared, coming around the corner, struggling to carry a big, bulky spool of something. Seeing her caught Boone off guard. When had she gotten so big? His little girl was gone and in her place stood a borderline adult. He could still remember the terrified look in her eyes when he'd found her tied to the totem pole at Camp Tall Pines a few months back, but looking at her now, that could have been a completely different person. She was still scared, sure. But she seemed hardened at the same time. There was a bite to her expression. As if all the blood that had been spilled around her had somehow seeped into her eyes, sharpened them.

"Nail gun seems dumb. There's a pressure point on the front that has to be pressed down and a whole air compressor that has to be running. It'd be a pain in the ass to get it to shoot something. BUT I found this."

Athena held up a spool of barbed wire.

"I didn't even know they had barbed wire here. This is country as shit, and-" Athena looked at the cart. "-holy crap. We're going full Home Alone here, huh?"

Boone looked at the cart, trying to refocus. But it wasn't working. The wheels were spinning. His baby girl was gone. Despite everything he'd done. Everything he'd tried. He'd lost his baby girl along the way. She'd grown up, thanks to his best efforts. There was no going back to princess tea parties, pigtails, or walks in the stroller. There was no going back to innocence. To naivety. To normal. Normal had grown up, evolved. Normal now was sacrificing their old lives to protect their new selves.

Boone swallowed the lump in his throat and made his peace with what was about to happen. To get through the night they were going to have to burn everything down.

"We're gonna throw everything at these bastards and the kitchen sink."

"You could probably actually throw the kitchen sink, couldn't you?"

"Without a doubt."

"Cool."

"And we're getting lawnmowers!"

"Fuck off, demon."

Athena tossed the barbed wire on top of the cart's pile.

"Alright. We've gotta go. Truck won't carry much more, and we've got some prep to do before the big bads show up."

Athena nodded.

"Any word from your friends?"

Athena glanced down at her phone. Read a new text.

"Meredith says Simon's been admitted and both of their parents are at the hospital now. She says they're calling our family a bunch of bad names. Pretty sure they're never gonna be allowed to come over again, but Meredith says nobody's called the cops yet."

"Good. Keep them out of this. We don't need any more collateral damage."

"Have you figured out how to get the cops outside of our house to leave yet?"

"We could just kill them."

"No. Fuck off, demon. One thing at a time here. First we've got to get home, get all this set up. Protect ourselves. Then we'll try to save everybody else."

"Killing is more fun."

"Trust me, Shevra. There's about to be plenty of killing."

Boone wheeled the cart with the squeaky wheel to the front of the store and thanked the gods below for the self-checkout options. Nobody needed to scan all these items at once for him. They would hit those little emergency buttons below their desks before the Hammonds ever left the store.

Boone paid and slipped into the parking lot right before closing, packed everything into the truck, and headed home to brace for World War three.

She had actually found them.

Shelley sat on the curb on the intersection of Magnolia and Pine, staring at her bloody hands, and smiling.

She was disappointed in herself for taking so long. If she had just been paying a little better attention, she could have recognized the demon more quickly. Stupid Mr. Collier. Distracting her. Popping up at the theater like that, making Shelley think he was using Athena like bait also. Making her think he was the monster.

If she hadn't been so focused on him, maybe she could have warned the others in time to save them from the massacre at the library.

But ultimately it didn't matter. She had found the demon. Brock was on his way. And once they subdued the beast, Elijah Hanson would have to grant her passage to Kansas. She would become part of the core group. At long last, it was coming together.

No. Not long last. Shelley hadn't been working on this for more than six months. The rest of the acolytes had been devoted to this cause for years. Decades even, some of them. But none of them knew what Shelley did. None of them had an 'in' with a Final Girl.

Screw those dead suck-ups and their 'years of service.' Shelley was the hot hand. Shelley was the new kid on the block filled with rage and drive and potential. Shelley was the one that would avenge her best friend Elena.

It still baffled her. How Athena had survived the Camp Tall Pines massacre. When the news reports broke, at first, Shelley had been so excited. Jolene had kept her promise. Shelley's commitment to the Order had actually paid off. The world was going to begin anew and she and her best friend would be queens, princesses among the top ranks. Everyone dead. One survivor. That's what the news had said at first.

But then they started to clarify.

Athena's name got leaked to the press somehow. Not Elena's.

The counselors were dead too. Not missing, like they'd planned. Dead. They had the bodies. The carcasses. The receipts. The plan which had been so carefully orchestrated had gone FUBAR and the only person who knew why, or how, was the mousey girl who sat in the back of class. The one who had tried to steal Shelley's best friend from her. The one who ruined everything.

Fantasies of a world without parents, without school bullies, without anybody to come between Elena and Shelley died off in a blitz of headlines and "This Just In"s, and Elena had been left, alone, abandoned. It wasn't fair.

But now here she was, the first drops of revenge drying on her fingertips. Brock and the others would be here in just a few hours. They had a long drive. All of the acolytes from a 50 mile radius were dead at this point, save for Shelley. She thought of her mentor, Jolene. Wondered what, exactly, had happened to her back at that camp. How had Athena managed to strike down somebody so bold, strong, and exciting? The coward overcoming a goddamn lion?

It didn't matter. Elena. Jolene. Their deaths wouldn't have been in vain. The new world order was coming. It had just needed Shelley to turn the key a bit farther.

Shelley stuck her finger in her mouth. Sucked on the pointer finger and let her eyes roll back in ecstasy as the sour, coppery taste of vengeance coated her tongue. By the end of the night, she would become a legend.

Chapter Thirty

Athena

Athena sat on the cold tile floors of her home, barbed wire in her hands, ready to be strung across the kitchen's doorway. They had successfully pulled past the two cops who were sitting guard, their truck stuffed to the gills with sharp objects and blunt force instruments. The cops had looked up and shot Boone a curious look, but he'd shrugged their gazes off.

"Fixing the place up, since we're gonna be stuck here a while. Or are we not allowed to do that?"

The cops had shrugged, neither of them particularly enthused about this job. Days of stakeouts had worn off their edge. If Detective Ramsey had been here, the Hammonds would have been called out for their purchases, but these two? They were just punching a clock.

Boone pulled into the garage and closed it behind them, immediately began siphoning the gas out of his own tank and sent Athena into the kitchen to try to string up the razor wire. She had been at it for an hour now, knocking nails into the molding around the door frame and carefully, tightly, weaving her trap together. It got routine after a while, and her eyes had strayed elsewhere, away from her work. Boone returned with an empty gas can and sat down at the kitchen table.

For whatever reason, Athena's attention stuck on the fan in the living room, watching its old, slow blades twirl around and around and around. She hadn't paid attention to the fan in years. Hadn't really looked at it since...ever. Who ever really looked UP in their house? The fan's blades were painted white. Nearly the same color as the ceiling had been painted. Helping them blend in, go unnoticed in the Hammond family's day to day lives. Mission accomplished. But Athena didn't want the little details to go unnoticed right now. She wanted to absorb them all. Wanted to remember every nook and cranny of this house. Every crack in the plaster. Every chip in the molding.

This was going to be their last night at home. Ever. Her dad hadn't said that. Not out loud. But it was blindingly clear that after tonight, after what was about to happen, they would never be able to come back here. Cultists aside. Police aside. Their plan might legitimately wreck the entire house. Bring every board and window pane crashing down, eliminating even the temptation to return. It would be a clean break from the past. Cut and run to...where?

"Dad? Where will we go after...this?" She tore her eyes away from the fan, found her dad fiddling with some nails and old lightbulbs at the dining room table.

"Dunno, baby. Where do you want to go?"

"Straight to hell?" The demon offered, and Athena threw a shoe at her dad and the demon's backside.

"Back off, Shevra. We're helping to release you again. Don't antagonize my dad," Athena called as the shoe struck them and her dad flinched.

"Are you? We gonna draw a sigil in the wolves' blood? Get thirteen of them rounded up and slit their throats again, just like camp?"

"I dunno. You're the expert in all of this. You tell me the best way to pry you out of my dad's body and I'll go get the damned crowbar."

Shevra laughed.

"I like her more this time. Have I said that yet? You're raising your little psychopath right."

"Shevra, could you let us talk?" The changes in inflection when Boone was in control versus when Shevra was in control were subtle. But they were there. A touch less menace. A bit more empathy. Things that only Athena would have picked up on, after listening to her dad speak year after year. Hundreds of 'how was your day's told over the dinner table.

"What about Seattle, sweetheart?" he asked. And it was him, not the demon, in control again. "We can switch coasts? Go somewhere with some ocean?"

"Boo. Too cold," Athena answered as she raised the barbed wire up and looped it over a hook that she had set. She pulled it tight, twisted it, looped it around the hook again, then unspooled another couple feet's worth of wire, crossing the doorframe to a hook on the other side.

"If we're going West Coast, why don't we go to California? LA? I could star in movies."

She attempted a hair flip, but her hair snagged in a barb and she hissed, pausing her shenanigans to untangle herself.

Behind her, either her dad or the demon chuckled.

"Too expensive. Too many hipsters. But okay, we want warm? We go to Mexico? Maybe Venezuela. We can look up Central American extradition laws while we drive.

"I thought the goal was to blend in somewhere. Dad. We're pale."

"Maybe we could work on that. Take turns tanning in the truck bed while the other person drives the interstate. Crisp up a few shades before we hit the border."

"Dad, I can't drive, and neither of us speak Spanish."

"Buzzkill," Boone said around a chuckle as he tightened the base back onto a lightbulb he had just dismantled.

"I like that word. Sounds like murder hornets. Remember murder hornets, Athena? I found them in your dad's head. They sound like fun." Shevra said through Boone. "Speaking of which, where's the buzzsaw?"

"Calm down, demon...and it's already in position by the front door. Remember? Athena took care of that first."

"Yep yep. Hockey stick was just the right height and the extension cord worked well. I think I've got it rigged like you wanted, Dad, but could you check it for me when you're done with those...What ARE those?"

"Nail bombs."

"Gnarly."

"You guys. This is going to be so much fun," the Demon chimed in. "I'm just. I'm so proud of all of your hard work. You're doing such a good job."

"Are you patronizing us?" Athena asked, finishing with the barbed wire and using a pair of clippers to snip her work free from the rest of the roll.

"Okay, Demon. If you won't shut up, then at least say something useful. Talk through the plan again. Prove to me you know it," Boone demanded.

"Again?"

"Again."

Boone's body let out a sigh of frustration.

"The big dumb idiot wolves will come up to our house of horrors."

"Right."

"We will wait, like cowards, very quietly in the house while our traps thin the herd."

"Still correct. Key word quietly. We don't give away our position until there's just a few of them left. Enough for us to corral and to keep away from Athena."

"Right. Because we can't die, but she's fragile."

"Rephrase that."

"Because we can't die, but her meat sack pops and spills like every other human and we can't let her meat sack pop."

"Nope."

"Because she's your daughter and if anything happens to her then you'll find a way to kill us both."

"Right-o. A hundred points for the Demon."

"But once the idiots' numbers are down, you'll let me come out to play."

"Sure. As long as we keep them away from Athena."

"And then I keep the last one alive so we can get answers from them."

"Correct. That's important, Shevra. If we don't keep one alive, then we can't figure out why you got drawn back into me. Why your powers faded. We won't be able to figure out why these Cultists keep coming after me and Athena. We can't figure out how to get our lives back. You'll have to show restraint."

Shevra wailed and moaned through Boone's lips and Athena saw her dad's eyes roll.

"But then we leave here forever," Athena said, softly.

Boone looked around the house, nostalgia burning in his eyes, dulling the spark of Shevra's mania for just a moment.

"Yeah. Then we leave here forever."

Athena frowned. Her face tightened and she looked into the living room. At the couch she'd grown up on. At the recliner where she'd seen her father doze a trillion times. At the ugly-ass wallpaper that Boone had insisted on preserving.

"I wish mom was still here."

"Me too, sweetie."

Boone frowned and stared at the light bulbs for a moment before walking into the front hall. Athena heard glass being smashed and Boone returned, brushing shards from a picture. It was the picture of Athena as a baby, laying on her mom's belly at a picnic. In the picture, Boone stood beside them both with his arm out as he took the selfie. The crows feet around his eyes were gone. Athena's dad looked different in the picture. Better. Healthier. The scars and damaged skin, worn down from years of fighting fires (and cultists) looked younger, healthier. On the blanket, Athena's mom was radiant. Long, brown hair splayed out. The chaos of child rearing is forgotten, even just momentarily, as the giggle of a happy baby commanded the scene.

"Stick this in your pocket, kiddo. We're bringing your mom with us."

Athena smiled, sadly, and did as she was told, folding the picture carefully and then sliding it into the safety of her back pocket. A little memento of the past, sure. But also a reminder of everything that had been taken from her over the years. First her mom. Her best friend. Now her house. Basically every ounce of childhood that could be squeezed from her teenage body. Fate was an asshole. But maybe after this was all settled, Athena could start writing her own story. This was step one of Athena seizing her destiny back from the Gods who had toyed with her, stolen from her, for so long. What was this house, but a bunch of boards? Pipes? Wiring? Losing some structure shouldn't define her. She should define herself.

She tried to shift her mind off of the nostalgia pangs; tried to steel herself for what was to come. The photo of her family hung heavy in her pocket, safe, but out of sight. Out of mind. She could take it out whenever she wanted. She could put it back when she wanted. Her little, broken family sat compartmentalized. Tucked away, and Athena tried to make all of her emotions follow suit. The sadness she felt about a normal life being ripped away. The betrayal she felt, realizing that Shelley had just been using her. It all had to go. For now. Until the night was through. Until these cult members had been hacked apart, slashed apart, limb by limb. Then she could take the picture back out.

Athena forced a smile.

"Lets wreck some faces, right?"

"Right."

"Do we still have that ladder in the garage? I have an idea with the fan."

"Yep. It's racked above the truck, same as always."

"I'm gonna go grab it."

"You do that, sweetie. I love you."

"Love you too, Dad."

"Love you too, sacrifice."

"DEMON SHUT THE FUCK UP."

Chapter Thirty One

Shelley

It was 3:30 AM when the unmarked white van pulled up in front of Shelley, the double doors in the back popping open before it had completely come to a stop. From the bowels of the vehicle climbed nine masked figures, armed to the teeth with riot gear and an armory's worth of weapons. Their gear was all black. Their masks, still colored, but darker. Made from heavy metal instead of the cheap plastic that initiates received, these masks were made for war. A piece fashioned to look like the wolf's lower jaw swooped down, around each wearer's chin, protecting their entire face from whatever was about to come. They were a strike team. Ex-military, ex-cops, even an ex-MMA fighter, if the rumors were true, assembled in the aftermath of Camp Tall Pines for exactly this reason- to take out threats to the order.

"Shelley?" The first wolf from the mask asked, walking up. His mask was charcoal grey. Brock.

"That's me."

"Where are they?"

"Back of the neighborhood. There's a house offset from the others by a decent bit, back in the woods. 3034 Miller Grove Court. But they know you're coming."

"They know we're coming," Brock corrected. He glanced over his shoulder and whistled to a wolf with a shotgun and a dark brown mask. Dark Brown reached back into the van and pulled out some spare gear and a jet black mask. He held them out to Shelley without any sort of ceremony. They acted like this was the most regular thing in the world. But to Shelley, this was her graduation.

Her hands shook nervously as she reached out and took the mask. It was heavy. Well made with materials and colors that suggested badassery; that she be taken seriously while she fucked some people up. It wasn't a child's plaything like her old plastic mask had been. No. She was done playing dress-up. This was a uniform. She slipped the mask on and tightened the straps, allowed herself to revel in the moment for an instant before reaching across and taking the rest of the gear: a vest and some heavy black pants.

Brock watched the exchange quietly, half paying attention to Shelley, half issuing orders to the rest of the team with wordless flicks of his wrist and swings of his arm. Body language that Shelley wasn't trained to understand.

"What else do we need to know?" Brock asked once Shelley was dressed to kill.

"There's a cop car out front. Usually there are two policemen inside, but it's been quiet enough here that neither of them will be paying any attention."

Brock pointed to Charcoal and Blood Red, held up two fingers, then twirled them over his head like a flashing light. He drew a thumb across his neck and the other two wolves slipped into the darkness.

"Taken care of." He said it with a confident authority. Two people named, two people dead. It was as easy as that. "Nobody knows about the library?" he asked.

"Not yet."

"Entrances to the house?"

"Front door would be the most obvious choice, but there's a tree in the back that leads to Athena's window. We could sneak in through there."

"Athena?"

"The idiot that survived Camp Tall Pines."

"She's the vessel for the demon?"

"No. That's her father, Boone."

"Got it."

"How do I help?" Shelley asked, relishing the way the mask responded to her words, its mouth opening and closing smoothly.

"You don't. You stay in the back and you stay perfectly silent until you see something that's off."

Shelley frowned.

"I'm not a child. I can help."

"You literally are a child."

"I'm the only person that's seen the demon and lived. You need me."

"That's why you're tagging along."

"But I don't want you to put me in the back. Don't tell me to be quiet and speak when spoken to or any of that crap."

Brock groaned and made a few quick adjustments to his gear, unsheathing and resheathing the ornate knife on his belt, making sure that it came out quick and clean.

"You've got a high opinion of yourself, girl."

"Damn right."

Brock didn't let the conversation continue. He turned to the other five wolves, still lingering near the van and gave a thumbs up. Each of the other five gave him a thumbs up back, and Brock howled from beneath his mask, the cry echoing through the trees and off the night sky. Overhead some bats adjusted their course, steering clear of the neighborhood below. Feral cats hunkered down in the woods, and dogs let out low growls by their master's beds. Every living being in the sleepy town of Bayside, Virginia felt the tension in the air shift. Feeling what was coming deep in their bones. But only Boone, Shevra, and Athena knew the source of the feeling. Only those three were prepared, the last nail driven into the walls of Athena's childhood home, ready for the storm to try breaking the doors down.

Chapter Thirty Two

Team 1

The Wolves came through the trees from multiple angles. Three slid away from the cop car with its pool of blood collecting just below the driver's side door, moving noiselessly up the driveway. Four more came from the left side, through the trees and the overgrown vegetation. Three more came from the right side, following along a creek's path and keeping low, just like Shelley, Meredith, and Simon had done over and over again in the days leading up to this.

Clarissa led Team 1 straight up the driveway, a flashlight lit and fastened to the front of her shotgun like a bayonet onto a rifle. She moved slowly, scanning the ground in front of her for any sorts of traps. Tripwires. Alarms. Tiger pits full of punji sticks. She'd seen it all over the years, and knowing what they were up against had her on high alert.

But there was nothing.

The whole drive, up through the woods, was suspiciously calm.

The demon knew they were coming. That's what Brock had said in the van. So the decision not to set up some sort of a perimeter around their safe space was either exceedingly stupid or wildly arrogant, on their quarry's part.

Her right heel squelched as she walked, coated in the dead police officer from the road's blood. The sticky warmth acted like glue, picking up dirt and debris as Clarissa walked, and she dragged her foot along the dirt, trying to remove some of the detritus. The last thing she needed was a slick of wet leaves causing her to slip and fall as she turned, or a trail of muddy footprints showing the demon exactly where she was or wasn't going through their house.

Why, oh why, had she felt the need to finish the bastard cop off with a curb stomp?

To her left and right, her fellow wolves in their maroon and burnt orange masks froze, dropping to their knees beside her, guns up, eyes trained on the woods. To their left, Clarissa could still see Team 2 moving into position, but to their right, Team 3 was gone, dropped down, out of sight, down into the creek.

With her glove, Clarissa swept away the mess of leaves and little sticks. She rose and surveyed the house.

It looked like any other house in the suburban neighborhood. Set back from the others, sure. Surrounded by woods and trees that would help hide their approach, and dampen the sounds of the coming assault, the house was cookie cutter from every other suburban hellscape in the mid-Atlantic. Nothing would have suggested a Fallen Lord's presence inside. No bloodsoaked turrets or corpses on pikes lined the drive, like Clarissa had expected, half hoped for. It was just...quaint.

Clarissa moved up to the front porches' steps and felt her foot squelch again. Damnit. She had just cleaned her boots off. How were they still sticky?

She crouched again, lifting up her mask so that she could see better, and to her left and her right, Maroon and Burnt dropped to their knees again. Maroon's gun faltered on its way up and he looked down at his knee on the ground, confused by something.

The ground.

It wasn't Clarissa's foot that had felt squishy this time, it was the ground itself. Clarissa aimed her flashlight down towards her feet.

Dead grass lay in a foot-thick line all across the front of the house. Damp. Wet. Dead. Clarissa's foot had sunk a good inch down into the yard from the way it was soaked and, with her mask off, now Clarissa could smell the source of the dampness. She could feel it trickling down on her, Maroon, and Burnt Orange.

Clarissa jumped up and back, raising her gun and light towards the gutters overhead.

"Fucking Fuckers!" she hissed. Holes had been drilled into the gutters. She could see where the drainage pipes had been crimped closed, twisted shut, to make the gutters into a slowly leaking trough, and gasoline rained lightly down on Team 1.

"Elaborate," Brock said.

"There's. I dunno. Some liquid just poured all over us on the front porch. Like a...shit. That's gasoline. All teams stand down," Clarissa called. She ran her gloved hand over her body armor, checking to see how bad it was. Soaked wasn't the right word. But the gasoline was everywhere. Her armor had been compromised and, based on the way Maroon and Burnt both kept slapping at their own arms and legs, Clarissa had to assume they'd been got also.

"Taking off armor" Team 2's leader said in the radio.

"Negative, Team 2. Safety first," Clarissa called back. That idiot. He wanted to go fight a demon without any riot gear? Just because there was a little gasoline splattered about? No. Her team was going to keep their defenses up. They would just need to be careful; watch out for any open flames.

"I'm not going into that house covered in gasoline. Guaranteed they have a lighter somewhere just waiting to flick on. Removing armor now, taking our chances with light, fast, and non-flammable." Team 2's leader said, his thick Boston accent crackling through Clarissa's headset.

"Brock?" Clarissa asked, hoping the leader would take charge. Force Team 2 to behave rationally.

"Team 1, keep your armor on. Team 2, go light. We'll hedge our bets."

Clarissa groaned. Chalk Team 2 up to dead men walking. They'd be dead in minutes, then it would just be her and the upstairs crew trying to clear the house. She cursed Brocks' idiocy, but signaled to Maroon and Burnt to move forward.

They hustled through where the gasoline was trickling, hurdling over the puddle and landing on the porch, leaning up against the front door, Clarissa on the left side of the entryway, Maroon and Burnt on the right side. Burnt reached a hand out for the handle, but Clarissa shook her head 'No.'

After the gutters? Surely they would have rigged the front door with something. Better to try one of the windows along the front. Clarissa crouched down, trying to stay light on her feet as she approached the window near her left side and tugged on it, found it resistant, but unlocked, and the window reluctantly groaned open after a few moments of insistence. Burnt and Maroon came around, set their backs against the front wall and watched the front yard, guarding Clarissa's back as she put the nose of her gun through, then her head. She had entered the Dining Room. The Dining Room table was cluttered with a carousel centerpiece and a dozen lit candles. Clarissa scowled through her mask and unconsciously took a step back. "Open flames," she called back to Burnt Orange and Maroon. "Watch your step."

Clarissa glanced at her armor, still slick with gasoline from the gutter trap outside. She scanned left and right again, double checking that the candles on the table were the only, distant, threat, and then lifted her foot over and in, testing the hardwood floors inside to make sure there wasn't some trap waiting where she was about to step. Her boot found nothing but solid footing though, and Clarissa exhaled in relief before sliding the rest of herself inside.

"Inside. All clear," she whispered into her headset, still eyeing the candles nervously. Behind Clarissa, Maroon angled his way through the window and Clarissa kept her eyes peeled. There was a baby monitor in the China Cabinet to her left. There were no lights to indicate that it was powered on, but she could have sworn she saw it inch its lens around ever-so-slightly right before she heard the click come from the carousel.

The table's centerpiece, an ornate glass structure with horses and elephants and sleds arranged around its circumference crawled to life, music droning up from within it, played on some idiophone like a music box.

Ring around the rosie. Pockets full of posie.

Burnt Orange was halfway through the window now, struggling to get their heavier frame and their bulky armor through the threshold.

Ashes. Ashes. We all fall...

As the carousel spun, the bug spray came into view. An aerosol can, seated just below one of the horses, came around as the centerpiece spun and one of the porcelain horse's hooves came down on the trigger, compressing it, and sending a line of bug repellant spraying out, across the top of the candles.

Down.

Flames erupted, filling the room in a flash, the aerosol can having been weaponized like a flamethrower. Clarissa tried to dive out of the way, but there was nowhere to go- Burnt Orange was clogging the window and the only door leading from the room was on the opposite side of the table. Clarissa dropped to the ground, lying below the hose of flames and rolling around to try to extinguish everything. But the gasoline on her armor was tenacious. Within a few seconds, the flames had built up heat through her riot gear, and Clarissa hurriedly pawed at the buckles keeping her bulletproof armor on her torso. The clasps fell away and she freed herself from the burning wardrobe, casting it away quickly, her scorched under-garments and toasted skin screaming with relief as they were exposed to the open air.

Her mask, though. Wearing a metal mask had been a bad choice. The flames turned Clarissa's mask into a frying pan and she clawed at the buckles on the back of her head, trying to get the mask off her face before it got hot enough to sear her skin.

She was too slow.

When the clasps finally popped, allowing Clarissa to pull the mask free, she felt a patch of skin rip free from her cheek. The wound felt cold, and blood immediately gurgled forth to soak her chin and dribble down her throat to her exposed torso.

Pained, angry, and more than a little disoriented, Clarissa threw her burning mask at the carousel and saw it knock the aerosol can free from the compressing hoof's pressure. The flamethrower cut out, but the damage had been done.

Clarissa looked around at Maroon and Orange as she tried to find something to compress against the wound in her face. Maroon's mask had somehow gone unlit, but his torso and arms were fully ablaze. His hands scrambled through the flames, trying to unfasten the plastic clasps which had melted and fused together, holding the riot gear against him. He slapped at the fire with his hands, to little effect, and screamed like bloody murder as he baked.

Orange was still stuck in the window. He had gotten a face full of the attack and he flailed around, panicking too much to push free through the window, and Clarissa became woefully aware of the smells of burnt hair, and the sizzling sound of flesh popping whenever there was a lull in Orange's screaming.

Clarissa had won her battle with her damaged gear. The others, not so much. Clarissa's clothes smoldered against her, and she could see her skin, superheated and exposed through the damaged garments. Her skin had begun to blister and pop from even just the short 10, 20 seconds that she'd been on fire for. That was going to hurt in the morning, but it would be nothing compared to the pain Orange and Maroon were feeling. She debated which of them to help first.

There was an explosion. A thunderous boom that seemed to shake the whole house, and Clarissa dropped into the ready position, trying to locate the source through her ringing ears and her screaming, barbecued skin.

Orange, in the window, continued his screaming. He had managed to get one hand up to his mask, but couldn't quite remove it. He pulled and tugged at the flaming helmet and Clarissa saw dark, blackened skin forming around his neckline. His movements slowed. His head lolled to the side. He ceased to struggle, just letting his flame-drenched head slump into the house unsupported.

Dead.

But where had that boom come from?

Clarissa looked at Maroon, who had also stopped struggling with his burning attire. He stood still in the room with Clarissa, mask looking down towards his own blazing torso. One of his hands was soaked in blood. The hand that had been trying to beat the flames off of his bulletproof armor.

No.

Not the armor.

The weapons pouch on his armor.

As the flames continued to work, eating through Maroon's kevlar vest, superheating all of the shotgun shells and the pistol ammo which Maroon had packed for the trip, there was another explosion. Another bullet bursting, superheated gunpowder hurling a second shell from its casing.

"Help–" Maroon managed to beg before the drumroll from hell began.

The bullets popped in rapid, chaotic succession, and Maroon fell, spinning, to the floor, a trail of fire chasing him down. His body convulsed, kicking back and forth as a shotgun shell in his chest pocket exploded, throwing his shoulder backwards, then a pistol round near his hip popped, causing his leg to kick out wildly.

He shook on the floor, ammo firing over and over into, around, and through Maroon's body. The window beside Clarissa exploded as buckshot ripped a hole through the vest and escaped into the open air. More and more bullets followed, and before Clarissa had a chance to duck for cover, her exposed face popped. Three bullets found her, maskless, all at once, and she dropped to the ground as a limp, broken mass. Team 1 went radio silent.

Chapter Thirty Three

Team 2

It was the goddamn Fourth of July near the front of the house. Emilio and the other three wolves who had climbed through the kitchen window all hit the deck together, weapons clutched tight, heads whipping about, trying to figure out where the explosions were coming from.

To Emilio's right, the gas stove in the kitchen flickered, harmlessly. The can of bug spray which had waited for them, spitting condensed air and chemicals across the stovetop towards their team, sat empty. Unlike the carousel of death in the dining room, the kitchen's flamethrower-esque attack had surprised Team 2. But without a bunch of gas-soaked armor, they had managed to step back with ease, getting out of its range with little worse than a slightly singed shoulder for Emilio.

Now the can hissed at their squad harmlessly, like a dying cat.

It was a good thing Emilio had told his team to strip outside. Leaving their compromised wardrobe laying in the yard had let them clear the kitchen easily. Unlike Team 1, based on the mysterious explosions.

Emilio compressed the speaker button on the side of his mask.

"Brock? Something's wrong with Team 1."

"I know. We can hear it out here," Brock's reply came through the speaker, oddly calm. Like losing an entire third of their strike force was something to be expected.

"You and your team make sure you do your jobs. We'll find a different way into the house and meet up with you in a minute. Radio silence from here out."

"Roger that."

The radio clicked dead and the explosions from the front of the house stopped, just as suddenly as they had started. Emilio looked around, cautiously.

He and Bronze were the only wolves that still had their masks on, having miraculously kept them dry through the gas drip. But all four members of his team were vestless. Which meant their ammo was limited. Their bodies defenseless. They would have to be careful.

Emilio raised the pistol in his right hand and leveled it towards the front of the house, noting the way barbed wire had been pulled tight across each door frame. He turned to Charcoal mask, whose pale complexion now stood naked, like a ghost in the darkness. Charcoal had a serrated knife with him. Emilio pointed at the knife and pointed at the barbed wire. Charcoal nodded and set to work.

Blood Red, whose pistol had been abandoned outside, too gas-soaked to be trusted, began opening kitchen cabinets one at a time, looking for some other weapon he could use. This was the first time Emilio had ever seen Blood Red without his mask. He had a tight crew cut and scars all along the left side of his face. Straight lines criss-crossing back and forth across one another, made by some blade or another.

Emilio cringed each time Blood Red opened another drawer, expecting the explosions to start up again at any moment. Whatever had come after Team 1, he didn't want Blood Red's scavenging to trigger it for them. Emilio was about to say something when Blood Red stood up, a cast-iron skillet in his hands. He tested the thing's weight and shrugged.

"Seriously?"

"What?"

"Why don't you take a knife or something?"

Blood Red gestured at the empty butcher's block where the kitchen knives were absent.

"Any other great ideas?"

"Well that doesn't bode well," Charcoal groaned from near the barbed wire. He had made his way about a quarter of the way up the door frame, carefully peeling the jagged obstacle out of their way one strand at a time.

Bronze stepped up next to Charcoal and shone her flashlight through to the next room.

"Living Room" she whispered back to the others. "Looks empty. Like. Completely empty. There's no chairs or couches or anything. What the fuck?"

Emilio raised his finger towards his mask, wanting to call to Brock to ask if he had any insight, but remembered that, no. Radios were off. He glanced to his right, towards the front of the house, wondering if they should move instead in Team 1's direction. But those explosions...whatever had been going on up there made him nervous. They would have to go through the living room. But again, they would just need to be careful.

"I dunno," he said to Bronze. "Stay alert though. We move through the room fast. Be careful not to touch anything, and whatever trap they have set up, we'll just slide past it."

"I hate this. We should warn Brock. Back out. Let Elijah and Kansas know that the place is a deathtrap and reassess," Bronze suggested.

But the rest of the team wasn't having it.

Blood Red stepped up and shoved Charcoal out of the way. He squatted down and slipped through the opening that had been made in the barbed wire.

"We're not quitting on Brock, and we're not reporting back to Hanson without this thing in a bodybag. Quit being such cowards. It's some suburban teenager, her dad, and a handicapped demon. You're acting like goddamn Jigsaw himself rigged this place to blow. Come on. Let's find the demon, let's kill it, and let's get out of here. I'm done wasting time." Blood Red said back through the curtain of pointed steel.

Emilio glanced back towards the front of the house where Team 1 had died. He touched the dagger on his hip and nodded. He tried to swallow his nerves. Tried to act as tough as Blood Red was acting. But the shadows in this house felt like they were pressing in on him. His ears still rang from those explosions that took down Team 1. He wanted to turn back. He'd never wanted to turn back before, but now, here, actually in the presence of something so malicious as a demon, all of his fantasies of god-killing drained away. Reality took over. And he didn't like the reality of the situation.

Charcoal ducked through the opening in the barbed wire, followed by Bronze, and finally, Emilio. One of the barbs pricked at

Emilio's shoulder, through his shirt, and he cursed the fact that he didn't have his armor on. Maybe now that they'd cleared the kitchen with its open flame, they should turn back. Get their gear together again. But Blood Red was done being patient. He had already crossed the living room and found the doorway leading to the front hall. Like the door from the kitchen, this one was covered in barbed wire.

"Holy shit this is fucking tedious," Blood Red grumbled, and he waved a hand at Charcoal, motioning for them to come clip an opening for them.

"Hurry up. At the rate we're going it'll be daylight before we even clear the upstairs."

Bronze stepped up next to Emilio and shone their flashlight around the room along with him. The whole place was empty. Cleared out by the Hammonds. But why?

BEEP

Emilio's brows furrowed as Charcoal dropped to a knee near the barbed wire, set to clip their way through the bottom strand.

"What was that?" Emilio asked.

Blood Red turned, raising his skillet.

"What was what?"

"That beep. Somebody else heard it, right?"

"Yeah, I heard it." Bronze confirmed, adjusting her grip on her pistol, eyes going wide as she looked around the room.

Emilio glanced up, above the group, and saw the fan beginning to spin.

"Oh. Okay. It's just the-"

The fan picked up enough speed for the coils of barbed wire that had been hidden atop its blades to come slipping off. The wires had all been cut to different lengths so that as they tumbled down, and the fan blades spun faster and faster, the wires unfurled, stretched their prickly fingers out and out in an effort to kiss the edges of the room. With the furniture out of their way, there was nothing to get snagged on. Nothing to prevent them, to prevent the fan, from gaining speed, twirling faster and faster. Nothing, that was, except the unprotected bodies of the four cultists.

"Hit the deck!" Emilio screamed, but it was useless. One of the lengths of wire slapped him in the side of the face, a barb snagging on his ear and ripping a trench in his cheek as it pulled itself free.

Blood Red spun, showing his back to the wires just as three of the strands slapped at him. His shirt snagged and pulled, and the fan overhead groaned its motor straining to pull the barbs free. But it did. And the motor picked up more speed. And more speed.

Charcoal, still near the doorway that led to the hall, began hacking at the barrier in front of him frantically, trying to escape as the whirlwind of metal picked up enough steam to reach him, spanking him in the ass with razors and sending a splash of blood across the Hammond's carpet.

Emilio turned back to the kitchen door and, getting as low as he could, he began to crawl back towards the relative safety of the room they'd already cleared.

Bronze wasn't so quick on her feet.

She shrieked as the spinning barbs struck her over and over again, hacking away at her shoulders and arms, and Emilio heard a sick popping sound as one strand of barbed wire zeroed in on Bronze's soft, exposed flesh, whipping her in her belly over and over again as it twirled.

Charcoal looked up and thought fast, found the light switches beside the door frame and tried flicking both of them, to simply turn the fan off.

It was a mistake.

Electricity sparked through the device, trying to light the bulbs in their sockets, finding nothing but a booby trapped mess. The charges which Boone had planted in the bulbs got sparked and exploded, sending glass, nails, and screws flying around the room as four nail bombs exploded overhead.

Each of the cultists got peppered with shrapnel, Charcoal taking a nail to the throat, Emilio taking a screw to the kneecap, and all of them getting punched, hit, and cut so thoroughly that Emilio gave up trying to track his wounds.

Blood Red, unwilling to stay on the defensive for too long, tried to go berserker. He stood, all at once, and spun to face the fan, nails jutting from his shoulders and chest. He put his arms up in front of his face and charged towards the center of the death vortex. The barbed wire battered him, slashing at the left side of his body over and over as he battled forward, barbs digging into his head, his hip, his legs, wires wrapping themselves around Blood Red when they couldn't dislodge themselves, the fan continuing to spin, winding them around Blood Red's extremities in a grotesque, affront to both physics and anatomy.

Blood Red roared, covered in barbed wire, and, in a last-ditch surge of desperation and violence, Blood Red seized some of the wires around him and pulled.

Overhead, the fan came to a halt. Emilio smelled the motor burning up, trying to keep spinning as the burly, lacerated man below raged against the machine with his waning strength. There was a crack. A splitting noise as the screws and bolts that held the contraption against the ceiling gave way and the fan fell.

Bits of plaster, barbed wire, metal, glass, and wood all rained down together as Blood Red won, his rage against the machine liberating it from its high ground.

Bronze hadn't been paying attention. On her knees, clutching her stomach to try to keep the blood in, Bronze was woefully unaware of the fan that came crashing down onto her. Maybe that was for the best. Getting brained by a ceiling fan, its base splitting your skull open in a single blow, seemed like a relatively quick way to go.

Quicker, at least, than Blood Red's end.

Blood Red lay, trapped beneath a sheet of barbed wire that had collapsed on him. Each of his arms and legs were bound by the razor wire, and from what Emilio could see, there wasn't a single spared inch of flesh that wasn't split and gushing blood. The pool of crimson around him grew like somebody had turned a bloody faucet on, and as he died, Blood Red moaned; tried to speak, but the wires digging into his chin kept his mouth clamped shut.

Emilio crawled back through the gap in the barbed wires, into the kitchen. He rose, his head and flashlight still facing backwards, at the destruction he was escaping. He didn't see Boone Hammond until it was too late.

"Handicapped demon, huh?"

Boone and Shevra's warped, duplicated voice growled from right behind Emilio who turned to face the pair. Boone looked bigger than he had in the profile Emilio had been given. Maybe it was the demon's influence, causing his muscles to bulge, his frame to expand. But his eyes shone, even in the darkness, with an inhuman fury.

"We prefer the term handicapable."

Boone kicked Emilio in the chest with a strength that defied logic. Emilio's sternum snapped on the impact and he flew backwards, through the remaining barbed wire in the kitchen doorway. Some of the barbed wire came loose, collapsing to the ground along with Emilio's body. Some of it held tight, the nails in the door frame proving resilient, the metal unyielding, and chunks of Emilio's body were ripped clean away. Sections of scalp. An ear. Three fingers. Bits of Emilio scattered in every direction as Charcoal screamed from her position near the other doorway and Boone stepped through the opening they had made, lumbering towards the last remaining member of Team 2.

Chapter Thirty Four

Team 3

Shelley led the team on the right side, keeping her eyes peeled for anything that looked different about the creek. Was that root different from the night before? Had that stump always been there? Where was the demon? Where was the father? Were those police officers in the car really all the security they had in place?

Shelley tugged on the straps that held her body armor in place, adjusted her mask as she crawled below the gap in the Hammond's fence and stood, officially within their property line. The backyard was littered with the Hammond's furniture, as if they were having the most expansive yard sale ever. Their couches, end tables, recliner, TV, and everything in between lay scattered across the lawn, discarded, seemingly, haphazardly. The house itself sat, dark and still on the other side, as if everybody inside was asleep. Shelley knew better, of course, but it felt so surreal; so odd to actually be sneaking in this time, after Athena had welcomed her through her window so many times before. Shelley looked up at Athena's window now, and saw it slightly cracked. An invitation. A subtle little signal from Athena to Shelley.

"I know you're coming. You know that I know that you're coming. So here. An opening. For old times sake," that crack whispered.

Shelley smiled and pointed. Brock, rising beside her, scanned the back of the house.

"That window's your usual way in?"

"Yep."

Brock shook his head.

"It'll be a trap." Instead, he pointed at a window on the first floor, towards the left side of the house. The living room, if Shelley's mental map was right.

Brock thumbed a button on the side of his mask and Shelley heard static chirp in her left ear. Brock's voice, gravelly and electronic, whispered to her.

"Team 3 in position. Back of house. Team 1? Team 2?"

"Team 2 in position," a man's voice laced with a heavy Boston accent said.

"Roger that. Team 1?" Brock asked.

A pause. No answer. Shelley turned towards Brock to see if she could see any panic or discomfort in his body language. But Brock stood perfectly still. A statue in the night.

"Team 1?" Brock repeated, his voice remaining calm and collected.

"Fucking fuckers…" a new voice grumbled.

"Elaborate," Brock said.

"There's. I dunno. Some liquid just poured all over us on the front porch. Like a…shit. That's gasoline. All teams stand down," the woman's voice directed.

"Shit!" The Bostonian's voice popped on the radio. "Same here. Gas. Dripping from the gutters seems like. Boots are soaked. Outer layers compromised."

Brock's flashlight rose, following the gutters along the back rim of the roof until he found what he was looking for. Above the back door, small holes could be seen drilled into the gutter. Something dripped down off the gutters, despite the fact that it had been weeks since it rained last, and a small puddle was forming below, ringed by dead and dying grass.

"Taking off armor," Team 2's leader said on the radio.

"Negative, Team 2. Safety first," Team 1's leader called back.

"I'm not going into that house covered in gasoline. Guaranteed they have a lighter somewhere just waiting to flick on. Removing armor now, taking our chances with light, fast, and non-flammable."

"Brock?"

"Team 1, keep the armor on. Team 2, go light. We'll hedge our bets."

There is a moment of silence over the radio as both teams consider the order.

"What are we doing?"

"Not walking through that like a bunch of fucking idiots," Brock's response came dripping with snark and disdain for his fellow team leaders.

Shelley nodded and, staying as low as possible, hustled towards the couch, using it for cover and dropping low. Brock and the other wolf, wearing a dirt brown mask, spread out wide, heading for a recliner and an end table for their cover. It was just as Brock flinched, ready to move out from behind the recliner, that they heard the explosions from the front of the house.

Brock raised his fist into the air, signaling for the others to stop. They listened as the gunshots rattled the house, waiting for their headsets to crackle to life, for anybody to make the "We got 'em" call. But the headsets stayed silent.

"Damn it," Brock growled, just loud enough for Shelley to hear.

They kept moving forward, towards the Living Room, but it wasn't until Shelley tripped over the Hammonds' sofa table that she realized the mistake they were making.

"Brock!" she yell-whispered.

Brock froze, dropped to a knee, and turned to face her. Brown did the same.

"What?" Brock hissed, his frustration at being interrupted apparent.

"The window. The one we're going towards. That's the living room."

It took Brock a moment to realize why that mattered, but then Shelley saw the leaders' mask turn to assess all of the furniture surrounding them. He hung his head in annoyance. Gestured for Brown to turn, to head towards the tree like he had originally called for. As they did, they heard Team 2's screams break out on the other side of the window they had just been approaching.

Another boom echoed through the night. This one less a gunshot noise, more a noise like something breaking. Snapping. Collapsing. They heard members of Team 2 shouting, crying out for help, but Brock ushered Shelley and Brown away from the window quickly, abandoning the others.

"Up, up, up" he demanded, and Shelley led the way up the tree, pulling herself from branch to branch, following the familiar route around the trunk, towards the suspiciously cracked window.

Shelley stopped when she got close to the glass. Inside the room, Athena's TV was turned on. One of the movies they had watched the other day, CURSE OF THE REAPER, was well into it's final act. Howard Browning stalked his prey through a cornfield, practical effects dripping off his face as he grew closer and closer to his final victim. Above the television, written in lipstick on Athena's bedroom mirror, Athena had scribbled

'Like Wolves To The Slaughter.'

Shelley had to smile.

Behind her, Brock drew his knife from the pouch on his hip and he maneuvered around Shelley to open the window fully, letting himself inside after giving the space a cursory check for threats. Shelley watched him, a chill running up her spine. But it wasn't a chill of fear. It was ice in her veins. Cool, cold, anticipation. Athena thought she was so safe in here. With her father. With her demons. She was probably bundled up somewhere, cowering in her little corner, thinking that the deaths of the distractions downstairs were some sort of a victory.

She didn't know what Brock had up his sleeve. In his hand, as it were. How could Athena know? How could Mr Hammond know? How could the demon, for that matter? It would be their little secret until the guillotine dropped.

And here Athena was, leaving little messages. Taunting Shelley as if she were the one in danger. Athena was about to learn. Shelley would show her the true strength of the cult of Elijah Hanson.

Wolves loved slaughters.

Wolves feasted at slaughters.

Shelley slid in the window, Brown coming through right behind her.

She looked down at her bare hands and considered picking up something for a weapon. Athena's childhood cheer baton? Maybe the curling iron from her dresser? Both were heavy enough to do some damage, but not to a demon. She opted to keep her hands free. She would just stay close to Brock.

"Come out, come out, wherever you are," their Team leader called as he slowly turned the knob to leave Athena's room, the yellows and reds from the TV flashing as The Reaper carved through his final victim. Brown dropped low, checking under the bed as below them, through the floorboards, the house sat perfectly silent. No footsteps from Team 1 or Team 2 scouting the location. No sounds as dying members of the other squads called out for help. It was as if Team 3 were the only people on the mission.

Brock stepped from the room and checked up and down the hall. He motioned back to the others for them to follow, and Shelley did, but Brown stayed put.

"There's something back here."

"Is it a teenage girl or her possessed dad?"

"No, it's a-"

"Then I don't give a shit!"

Brock slipped away, into the hall, and Shelley hurried after him.

"Like a snake or something. Did your friend have a snake?" Brown called from behind them, and Shelley's eyes shot open, horrified. Memories of the tentacled thing that had pulled itself from the library's basement still burned fresh in her mind. Shelley caught up to Brock and shoved him, trying to urge him faster down the stairs.

"Run," she shouted.

Behind them there was a deafening ripping sound as the flooring of the Hammond Home's second story got torn apart, Brown screaming in fear and surprise as the black, wriggling thing they had been investigating turned out to be the tip of a demonic appendage.

The wall that separated the steps from Athena's bedroom shuddered once, twice, then exploded as Brown's body was sent flying through the drywall, plaster raining down on Shelley who ducked and threw herself down the stairs.

Brock let Shelley go flying past. He had spun, halfway down the stairs, and crouched down into a ready position, like a wolf about to pounce at its prey. In his hand, the knife he wielded looked small, comedic compared to the shotguns, the chainsaws, or the scythes that Shelley had seen other cultists brandish. But looks could be deceiving, and Shelley knew better than anybody what that little blade was capable of.

Two tentacles, as thick as arms, reached through the hole that Brown's body had created, exploring the stairwell as the rest of Boone's body caught up.

Brock took a step forward, curling his body until one of the tentacles was level with his shoulder, and he struck. The knife bit through the tentacle with ease, and a splash of neon orange demon's blood burst forth, splashing across both Brock, and Brown's corpse, crumbled along the stairs.

"What the shit!?" a pair of voices screamed from Athena's bedroom.

Boone Hammond's casual, menacing pace was abandoned and he ripped his way through the wall, exposing himself to the cultists huddled on the stairs. Boone and the Demon glared at their wounded tentacle for the slightest of moments before turning their rage towards Brock.

"What did you do!?"

They threw themselves down the stairs recklessly, a half dozen new tentacles sprouting from between their fingers and lashing at Brock. But Brock danced around his whiplike assailants, tracing patterns in the air with his knife and catching the tentacles here, then there, bloodletting like a dancer in a shower of neon rain.

Shelley stumbled towards the living room, barely noticing the barbed wire in time to dive beneath it, landing on the corpse of Blood Red, but rolling off of them quickly. Jagged pricks of metal bit her skin through her clothes as she rolled and stumbled through the living room, but she refused to slow down as the battle behind her gained intensity, Boone and Shevra laying waste to the kitchen with a few powerful swings of their girthiest appendages.

The doorway to the front hall had been cleared for Shelley, with Charcoal Grey's body lying near the front door, a trail of strung out metal trailing them. To Shelley's left was the door to the basement. As soon as Shelley saw it, she knew that's where Athena would be cooped up.

"My dad's building a panic room. To keep me safe when the Cultists come back," Athena had said, trusting Shelley all those weeks ago. Gods, July had been arduous, hadn't it? Slowly building up

Athena's trust in her, bit by bit. Pretending not to care that such a boring little shit had made it out of the massacre when Jolene, smart, motivated, capable Jolene, had been left behind to be eaten by worms.

But Shelley's patience had paid off in the end.

"What is that knife?" Boone and Shevra screamed in unison as Shelley heard more wood splitting, more metal snapping. There was another scream from the demon, and though Shelley was smart enough not to look back, to see how Brock was doing, she had to assume he was picking away at the monster. Slowly chipping away at whatever counted for a demon's health bar.

Shelley tried the handle to the basement. Locked. Of course. So Shelley took a step back, spun around, and donkey-kicked the barrier with all her might.

The door shuddered, but stayed put.

Shelley tried again. Then again.

"Little pig, little pig. Let me come in," she called as she kicked one more time. The bolts which held the door shut cracked and broke through the molding on the back side and the door flapped open, revealing the staircase to darkness behind them.

Athena would be right down there.

There was another scream from the kitchen. This one decidedly more human than the warbled double-tones of Boone and Shevra's screams. They had gotten the better of Brock.

As if to punctuate the thought, Brock's body flew forward, landing on the ground right next to Shelley's feet. The knife had slammed between the Cultists's eyes, punching a slit through his mask.

Blood poured freely from the mask's eye sockets and down, past its jaw line.

Shelley allowed herself one glance over her shoulder, towards the kitchen, and saw Boone hunched forwards, clutching his gut in pain. Severed tentacles twitched on the ground around him, and the walls had been painted with the demon-human hybrids insides. Boone's right arm hung, limp, at his side.

"Fix this," he yelled to himself.

"I'm trying," came the response.

Shelley took a knee and grasped the knife, tried to wrench the weapon free. It had worked. Just like Elijah Hanson said it would. The ritual dagger could take life just as well as it had given it. Shelley thought of Hal. Why hadn't he used his knife to kill Shevra the first time she emerged? Why was it falling on Shelley, here, now, to do the job?

It didn't matter. All the glory was coming to her, and who was she to question the fates' methods. If she could just get the knife unstuck.

The weapon was buried to the hilt in Brock's face, his face completely, fully busted underneath, and some combination of his mask and his brain matter gripped the end of the blade tight, refusing to let go.

"Dad?" Athena called from downstairs, and Shelley was filled with pride. She had been right. Everything was lining up perfectly. If she could just... get... this... knife.

Shelley saw Boone perk up at the sound of his daughter's cry for help. Stumbling a bit, his legs not working the way they were supposed to, he tried to charge at Shelley. She saw Boone tear through a few strands of barbed wire, tearing them free from their moorings in the wall without so much as flinching.

She needed to move.

Shelley grabbed Brock's body and dragged him, and the knife, into the basement along with her.

She made it three steps down the stairs before the ground fell out from under her. Shelley's knee snagged against something in the darkness as she fell. String? Rope? A trip wire.

Electric motors spun to life, the Hammonds' final trap triggered, and Shelley tumbled down into whatever hell awaited.

Chapter Thirty Five

Athena

Athena sat in the corner of the basement, staring at her old baby monitor, switching from camera to camera, and tracking the battle as well as she could. She saw the three gas-soaked cultists enter the dining room and pressed the button on her remote to activate the carousel. She saw the four armor-less cultists enter the living room, and she activated the fan through her phone app. Everything had been going according to plan until Shelley showed back up.

The wolf Shelley had brought with her was flashing something around, it was hard to see through the tiny baby cameras, but whatever they wielded was hurting her dad. Hurting Shevra. Damaging them in ways that weren't instantly repaired by Shevra's weird demon magical biology tricks. She watched in horror, hand clamped over her mouth, as her father bled, and bled, and bled. He'd told her before about how he'd been carved in half back at Camp Tall Pines. How he'd lay in the middle of the bonfire at camp, and how Shevra had stitched him back together like a tailor fixing a suit. But for whatever reason, this time, he just kept bleeding. Stumbling about, grabbing at wounds which remained open.

All three of them moved out of view of the cameras, and for a grave moment, Athena was left alone with her thoughts, straining her ears for any signs that her dad had bounced back, that he was recovering and winning. There was a thud. Then another, and another, and another, and Athena heard the door to the basement bang open.

"Dad?"

But the silhouette that came into view wasn't her father. It was too slender. Too small.

Shelley.

She was dragging a body behind her, Athena couldn't know why. Didn't care. Athena smiled and looked at the spot on the staircase where she and her father had removed the steps, covering the holes with a runner from the kitchen and a tripwire that could activate the lawnmowers underneath.

Shelley stepped right through it. The tripwire was triggered. The upside-down lawnmowers leapt to life, and that should have been the end of Shelley. The end of the cultists. The end of the night for Athena and her family.

The lawnmower blades hacked at the falling bodies, slicing at the assholes' arms, necks, and torsos like a blender chewing up chicken legs.

But Shelley was like a goddamn cockroach. She wouldn't go down that easily. Shelley dragged the other wolf's body down along with her, tumbling around, and somehow landed on top of the other wolf.

The machines spit blood, skin, muscle, tissue, and bones every direction imaginable, but from the center of the geyser, Shelley came crawling. In her right hand, she still gripped the hilt of Brock's knife, its blade lodged in the older wolf's mask and skull. But now the mask and the skull had been liberated from the rest of Brock's body. Crimson dripped across the Hammond's basement as Shelley rose and took a step towards the closest wall.

She sneered at Athena, screamed, and bashed what remained of Brock's head against the brick wall beside her until the knife came free.

Now Athena recognized the blade. She had seen it at Camp Tall Pines only briefly, but it was the same knife, or at least looked like the same knife, that one of the wolves had used to commence the bloodletting at Camp Tall Pines. That was what had hurt her dad upstairs? Some ritual knife?

Shelley took a step forward and used the back of her empty hand to flick a bit of the other Wolf's skin from her cheek. Her tongue raced about, lapping up traces of blood from her lips and she pointed the knife at Shelley with hate oozing from her glare.

"So here you are again. Hiding while the big kids do the real work all around you. Pa-fucking-thetic."

"Shelley, stop. You don't know what you're-"

"I don't know!?"

"You...don't..." Athena looked desperately back towards the stairs. Where was her dad?

"Listen here, you pathetic little worm. I know exactly what I'm doing. So did Jolene. So did all of those cultists upstairs. They all knew what they were doing because they paid attention. They did the work. They knew there was more to this world than we were being led to believe, and they found Elijah Hanson, and they did the fucking work while you buried your head in the sand. You and your meddling father. Do you have any clue how much we all sacrificed for just a chance to bear witness to the eternals? The Fallen Lords? To be in the presence of one of their kind has taken the order centuries. And here you are. Telling me I don't know."

Shelley stepped forward quickly, closing the gap between Athena and herself before Athena had a chance to react. She pressed her blade against Athena's throat, its edge sharp and cool against her soft skin. Athena felt the warm trickle of her own blood running down her neck, down her chest.

"To be possessed like your father is. To receive the gift of a Fallen Lord inside of your own flesh. And that fool carved her out the first time. Discarded the gift that the eternals had bestowed upon him. Well I won't make the same mistake. Once I split their souls apart, I am going to relish my new position."

"Girl, you're too crazy even for me."

Shevra's tentacle leapt from the darkness, slamming Shelley to the side as other tentacles lowered Boone down, safely past the lawnmowers, into the unfinished basement alongside the others.

Shelley flew away, but never lost her grip on Athena's arm. She landed with the blade pressed still pressed against Athena's throat.

"Try that again and she dies, right here, right now."

Boone's feet landed on the concrete, and he teetered like a drunk. His eyes were unfocused. Orange ooze continued to leak from him in the bucket-loads.

"Dad?"

"Shut up."

"I'm okay, sweetie. You just worrybout you." Boone's words slurred.

"Aww. What's wrong, papa bear? Weren't expecting the fragile little cultists to come packing this time? To come prepared when we knew what we were dealing with? A traitor. An outcast. I'm talking to you, demon!"

"Who are you calling an outcast? You haven't even been accepted by this cult you're so high and mighty about yet. Now why don't you step away from the innocent little meat sack so we can finish this ourselves?"

"And let her just skate through another massacre? I don't think so."

It was hard for Athena to speak. Every time she took a breath, Shelley's knife dug a little deeper into her throat. But she forced the words out anyhow.

"You're right," Athena spit, and she felt Shelley tense behind her.

"I'm done being a passenger. It's my turn."

Athena spun around to face Shelley, blowing through the knife at her throat. She felt the blade slice through her skin. But she told herself not to care. Adrenaline let her block out the pain, only for a moment, but a moment was all she needed.

Athena seized Shelley by the wrist and stole the knife from her surprised, loose grip.

Up, around, down, the blade spun, and Athena buried it between Shelley's ribs.

Shelley's eyes went wide behind her mask.

"You little bitch…"

Athena shoved again, then again, forcing the knife deeper and deeper through Shelley's innards until Athena's first kill lost her balance and fell, collapsing to the floor, with Athena dropping beside her.

The two kids collapsed into a puddle of arms, legs, and spurting blood.

Boone and Shevra hobbled up behind them, throwing Shelley's corpse to the side and pulling Athena up into their lap.

"No, no, no," Boone wept as he tore his tattered shirt away, wrapping it around his daughter's throat and applying pressure.

"It's not that deep. It's not that deep." He said the words like a prayer, hoping them to be true more than he believed them.

Athena grabbed her dad's wrists, clinging to them like life rafts as the pain in her throat pulsed through her over and over. It hurt so bad. But she didn't think she was dying. How could you tell that? How could you know? Was there supposed to be a bright light or something?

She opened her mouth and tried to speak.

"It...I think...she missed..."

The words flowed up, through her throat without obstruction. She took a deep breath, found herself able to do so without choking on her own blood.

Boone pulled the scrap of his shirt back, just for a moment, and with the curtain of blood removed, he could see the cut itself.

"It got you on the side of your neck, baby. Not across the throat. It must have missed its mark when you twisted around."

The wave of relief Athena felt, knowing she wouldn't die, was short lived.

"Baby girl?"

"Dad?"

"I need you to grab this cloth for me. I don't think I can-"

Boone slumped backwards, his grip on his tattered shirt going limp, and Athena forced herself to sit up, catching the cloth successfully, but missing her dad's hand. Boone collapsed back to the concrete, eyes still open, but no longer alert. His gaze had drifted off, and he stared across the room towards where all of the drywall sheets were propped up.

"Baby? Girl? Get rid of my box."

"What box?" Athena pushed the pain in her neck away. Pushed away any thoughts of cultists or Shelley or sacrificial knives.

"The box..." he raised a finger, slowly, and pointed across the concrete towards the drywall sheets. Athena didn't understand. Maybe it was the pain in her neck, or maybe Boone wasn't making sense. She'd sort that out later. But Athena's eyes darted around, taking in just how much blood was in the basement now. How much of the blood was that older Cultist's? From the lawnmowers? How much was Shelleys? Or hers? Most important, how much was her dad's?

His face was pale and Boone's breathing was slowing more and more.

"Destroy the box...live your life...this...all...behind you."

His hazy eyes found Athena's again, and a small smile spread across his lips, despite the knife marks which criss-crossed his cheeks. That older Cultist had hit him again, and again, and again, with the weapon. Athena was just now realizing how many cuts her father had collected across his body. She tried not to look. Tried to just maintain eye contact with her dad. Something in her gut told her that was the most important thing right now. Just to be there with him.

"No!" Boone screamed, but it wasn't his voice again. Shevra railed against the prospect of death. "This is not how I go out. Not tied to some stupid, fragile, human."

Boone's back arched spasmodically, his hips jumping a foot into the air as a dozen tentacles burst from his back all at once. His shirt fell completely apart, revealing the extent of Shevra's infestation. Human skin molted away, exposing ripples of demonic rot laid over bones that had shifted, popped, broken and been shoved out of place. Shevra's true form shoved her face against the back of his exposed ribs, and Athena cringed at the sight of the Fallen Lord. She turned her eyes back to her father, grabbed his cheeks in her sticky, bloody hands.

Boone wasn't moving. Wasn't reacting. Not on his own, at least. The only part of his body that he seemed to have control of anymore was his face. He kept smiling through the pain. Looking at his daughter.

A single tear slipped from his eyes as Shevra bucked beneath him, trying to create separation from his fading life force.

"Athena! Take me in. We can kill them all together. We can avenge your dad."

"Avenge?"

"Baby girl. No. Leave all....of....this. Get a fresh start."

"There are no fresh starts. Not with them out there. And you're too weak to take them on yourself, girl. Come on. You know what I can do. Open your mouth, girl. Open your mouth!"

Boone shook his head, 'No,' and closed his eyes. His arms reached out, found Athena's shoulders, and she felt him squeeze her, tight, with the last bit of his strength.

"Girl...Athena...you can't do this alone." the Demon whispered in her ear, through her father's lips.

A small tendril slipped from Boone's ear.

Weak, fragile, it crawled across Athena's chin, toward her lips. It forced its way into her mouth, slime-covered tip brushing against her tongue, and-

Athena bit down on the parasite that had infected her father. With a growl that turned into a scream, she ripped with her teeth and tore the tentacle in half, spitting it across the room in a gush of spit, demonic neon goo, and blood.

Mess dribbling down her face, Athena kept screaming. Her sounds were wordless. Just the piercing cries of unmanageable emotion.

She wept.

Wept from the pain. Wept from the anger. Wept from the sadness.

The whole night, the whole year, caught up to Athena at once and she squeezed her father's limp form with every ounce of her strength, willing him to wake back up. But his head rested on her shoulder, unmoving. Shevra's tentacles lay motionless.

Athena sat in the dark basement for what seemed like years, trying to avoid the realization that she was alone.

Completely, totally, utterly alone.

Chapter Thirty Six

Detective Ramsey

The detective looked up from the tape recorder and met Athena's eyes for the first time in hours. Although they had been sitting in the hotel room together, they hadn't said a word. They had just listened, together, to the sounds of Athena's father slipping deeper and deeper into madness.

No. Madness wasn't the right word. Despite every logical bone in his body, Detective Ramsey finally had to accept what was happening here. This wasn't madness. This was possession. Honest to God, possession. He'd heard it. He'd seen it. He couldn't deny his own judgment anymore.

He thought he'd seen everything at the Summer Camp, but the things that had happened to the bodies in that house? There was no way a dad and his kid could have pulled that off. And listening to the man argue with himself on the tape? This wasn't some dissociative disorder. This wasn't multiple personalities or anything like that. Damn it all, this was real. And the girl sitting across from him had endured all of it.

He had found her at dawn, all alone, in the basement of her home. When Barton and Jones had failed to make their scheduled check-in on the radio, Ramsey had gone out to investigate personally. Found the crime scene.

He still couldn't explain why he hadn't followed protocol. He should have alerted the rest of the force immediately. He should have collected the survivor and brought her to the hospital to be examined.

But he hadn't. Some second sense of his told him to keep this all under wraps. Keep it need-to-know for as long as possible.

There was no telling if it was the right call yet.

"Your turn, girl."

"Athena. Only my demons call me, 'Girl.'"

"Whatever. Just talk."

"You heard it for yourself. You saw it for yourself."

"But I want you to fill in the blanks for me. What the shit did I just listen to?"

"The demon. From Camp Tall Pines. She came back."

"Funny how you never mentioned a demon before."

"Funny how you gave a shit what I said before."

Detective Ramsey narrowed his eyes.

"Listen, punk. I can bring you to the station right now. Let all those officers see your face. See what you've been through. But based on what I'm seeing? I don't think you want that. That was your friend in the basement, wasn't it? I met her the other day. Seemed like you two were close before you, or your dad, drove a knife through her guts."

Athena just stared at him.

"So seeing her in that basement? It's got me thinking you don't have a real good sense of who these people are that are after you, do you?"

Athena's eyes dropped to the floor, and one of Detective Ramsey's biggest theories was as good as confirmed.

"I didn't think so. So if I bring you in to the station, how confident are we that there won't be more of those cult members there, waiting for you?"

Athena frowned.

"So here's what I'm proposing. We talk this through, here and now. You stop holding shit back from me, and I don't bring you out anywhere public where those wolf-masked fuckers might get after you."

Athena nodded and wrung her hands together. She really could have used a shower. She stank of gore and sulfur. Maybe Ramsey could use that as a lure to get her to talk. Safety and a shower. Deals from him didn't get much better than that.

"She came back to him because she was weak. Something happened. The ritual...I don't know. Un-completed itself somehow? And she needed him to survive. It makes no sense."

"Why doesn't it make sense?"

"I was the last sacrifice. And I'm fine."

"How were you the last sacrifice?"

"I died. At the camp. And my dad used a defibrillator to bring me back to life after the demon left him. So I don't understand why she came back now, months later."

"So the Camp Counselors were conducting some satanic ritual-"

"-Not Satanic."

"-Right. Demonic Ritual? Better?"

Athena shook her head, like there was no way she was having this conversation right now.

"And they had to sacrifice a certain number of people to summon the thing?"

"Thirteen kids, it seemed like. Killed through bloodletting in the middle of some weird pattern they drew in the ground."

"So they killed the rest of the kids. Kept thirteen of you around, then slaughtered you in this ritual circle?"

"Yep."

"And twelve died before you did."

"Yep. I don't see what you're getting at here."

"And nobody else died in that circle after they drew it?"

Athena's face went pale. He had triggered something. He could practically see an idea worming its way into Athena's mind. Some realization dawning on her.

"Is this demon what the Cultists were after?"

Athena shrugged.

"Seems like it. But they weren't really in much of a villainous monologue mood. Didn't walk me through beat by beat of their plan. They kept mentioning Kansas though."

"Kansas?"

"Yeah. I heard them mentioning Kansas through the baby monitor while they walked around upstairs. And Shelley talked about someone named Elijah Hanson."

"Okay. Kid, you just gave me a name and a location. We can work with that."

"We?"

Athena focused on the Detective again, looked up and met his eyes again. There was a fire in those eyes. Some dragon that had woken up since the last time Ramsey interviewed the girl. This version of Athena seemed just as likely to pour scalding coffee down his throat as she was to offer him a mug, like she had last time.

Ramsey smiled.

"We."

"Work with that?"

Ramsey nodded.

"I like seeing cases through to their end. And this? This isn't done yet. You seem like you've got a score left to settle, and honestly, I don't understand what I'm up against here." I could use the help of somebody that's knocked down two waves of these bastards before. You know things I don't. Maybe you can fill me in while we drive, but call me crazy, I tend to value having backup on my sting operations."

"We can't just go hunting bad guys in Kansas...can we? Aren't there protocols or something that you're supposed to follow?"

"Yup. But I've got the distinct impression that somebody botched the Camp Tall Pines cleanup on purpose. And now, seeing how deep the infestation of these fuckers are? I'm not super inclined to trust anybody in my line of 'protocol.'" Dollars to donuts, you aren't the only one surrounded by wolves in sheep's clothing.

Athena blinked rapidly, trying to process what was happening.

"What makes you think somebody botched the clean up?"

"How many cabins were there, Athena?"

"Thirteen."

"So how many counselors were there?"

"Thirteen."

Detective Ramsey nodded and pulled up his phone, thumbed through until he found an email, then showed Athena the phone.

Athena hesitated before reaching out to grab it. What she saw was a prepared speech from the chief of police from the county the Camp had been built in. Ramsey had it pulled up already, waiting to show it to her. He'd known this was coming. Known what she would need to see.

She scanned the statement, picking the numbers out as she went.

"56 campers dead."

Athena cringed, remembering the way their bodies had been tossed indiscriminately in the bonfire.

"1 survivor."

Smile for the cameras, Athena.

"12 counselors dead."

She paused.

"It's a typo," she said. "It has to be."

But Ramsey shook his head, no.

"We found 12 dead cultists scattered around that camp. And I promise you, we found every body there was. Dogs, grid-patterned searches, we even dragged the lake. We got them all. But there's one missing, isn't there? You wouldn't staff a summer camp with fewer counselors than there were cabins, would you?"

Athena looked over at the box of her dad's things and the box she'd found stuffed behind the drywall sheets. The box with folders upon folders of cultist information stashed inside, along with the tape recorder where he'd cataloged his 'sessions' with Shevra.

"People higher up the ladder than me called the search off. Tried to sweep the obviously missing camp counselor under the rug. Maybe that's why I was so hard on you and your dad. I was being lied to from every side, and I'm not about that. But you know, don't you? You know something."

Panic rose in Athena's chest. He was right that it didn't make sense. How could it? But some part of her knew what, or rather, who, the Detective's missing puzzle piece was.

Athena tore the lid from the box and flipped through the files, quickly finding the file she was looking for. It was right on top, as if her Dad had laid all the evidence out for her to find. As if he had known this was coming. Like Ramsey having the police report ready.

She showed the picture to Detective Ramsey, and he read the name slowly.

"Jolene Dubanik."

Detective Ramsey smiled, but it wasn't a kind smile; wasn't happy. It was a smile of anger. Frustration manifesting in a smile because what was being suggested was so ridiculous, so utterly impossible, that a person couldn't take it seriously. You just had to laugh all the way to the mad house.

"Never heard of her."

Athena's world ended.

Chapter Thirty Seven

Kansas

The bunker sat a quarter mile below the surface of Fort Scott Kansas. From up top, the only thing indicating life in the area was an old barn. It was downtrodden. Looked mostly abandoned. No roads led to the barn, and nothing else survived for fifteen miles in either direction. The barn sat there, isolated, and only those who knew to pay attention would have discovered it to be the entrance to the ant hill underneath.

The hive had one hundred and thirteen included. They had all arrived the same way. Indistinct white van, driving through the empty expanse of Kansas. Unloading people, no more than four at a time, to join the cause at it's core. Thirty-three rooms had been built, slowly, decade by decade, as the cult's activities grew and grew.

Today, the cult would take their largest step forward to date. They would cross a threshold which had eluded them for hundreds of years. A threshold which Elijah himself had begun to doubt existed in his later years. But Harper had never lost the faith.

He smiled as he looked at Jolene's body, naked, hung vertically, in the center of a five-pointed star, looking for all the world like she'd been crucified to the spot. Wires connected her to multi-million dollar devices, all dedicated to this one event. This one moment.

Her body had been stitched together as well as possible. But there were some things. Arms that had been ripped-in half, length-wise. Baseball-bat sized holes punched through her skull, that Harper could only do so much with.

At first, he'd been made when his crew brought this body back. Why her? Why not a corpse with a simple stab wound? A throat slit, or a neck snapped? Why the body that had been torn, so thoroughly, to shreds?

But now Harper understood.

Though her body had been cold for months, somehow he could still feel the wraith's energy pulsing from it. Anger. Madness. Impressions that he could only get in the middle of the night, when all was quiet, and it was just him and Jolene left alone in the deepest room in the complex. But impressions which were unshakeable, once he felt them.

She wanted to come back. She wanted to burn this world down, still. All she needed was a window. No matter how small that window was, or how impossible the odds were, this vile being would claw her way back up from hell. She just needed a hand to reach out. Some way to pull herself up.

And Harper could give her that chance.

He had recreated her mask for her. Taking the fragments that his crew had retrieved, resealing them with gold, the way the Japanese did. Kintsugi. What is broken is never truly gone. Just waiting to be reformed. Embraced again.

Harper patted Jolene on the cheek. Reached in and kissed her blue, restitched lips.

Together, they would remake the world, as promised, he thought. And as he left, he turned out the lights.

Soon, he thought.

So very, very soon.

A Note From The Author:

Thank you so much for reading KILLER BE KILLED: HOMEWRECKER. Like with the first book in the trilogy, I had a stupidly fun time writing this pulpy, violent literary release valve for myself. I had the idea to do a bit of a tour-de-slashers after the Camp Slasher kicked things off for us, and a Teenage/Home Invasion Slasher felt like the natural next progression for things. I knew Athena needed to be thrust into the limelight this time. That she was going to have to evolve from the professional hide and seek role she had in the first book, and I hope that this felt like the nudge she needed to go completely, wildly apeshit in our conclusion. Keep your eyes out for Killer Be Killed: Blood In Their Eyes to drive the final stake home in 2024. There are so many more bodies for us to dismember.

If you feel so inclined, it would mean the world if you could leave a review on Amazon, Goodreads, StoryGraph, Bookbub, and/or anywhere else you frequent!

For our Friends on eBooks, here's a direct link to the William Sterling Author Page: https://www.amazon.com/-/e/B077CCC38C

Other books by me include:
Through Frozen Veins- Closed Room Supernatural Horror Mystery

Through Withered Roots- Small Town Disappearances Horror

Synapse- Dystopian, Memory Selling Horror

String Them Up- Coming September, 2023 from Crystal Lake Publishing- Murder Puppets and Small Town Horror.

Stay Spooky.
William Sterling.